A STRANGE WAY TO FIND LOVE

"What you want," Vanessa said aloud to Samson, "is a good evening meal which you shall have whatever it costs and a drink of pure water."

Samson pricked up his ears as she was speaking.

Then she passed through another field, which was, she thought, quite narrow.

At the far end of it there was another wood.

Beyond that would be the village and she hoped somewhere comfortable for the night.

The gate was open and she rode from the field she was in towards the next gate.

It was then she saw that the wood was narrower than she had expected and she could see trees just ahead of her.

Seated underneath the trees with their horses not too far away from them were a number of men.

She thought that they must be working in the field.

Then, as Samson carried her rapidly towards them, she suddenly became aware with a shock that they were highwaymen!

THE BARBARA CARTLAND PINK COLLECTION

Titles in this series

1. The Cross Of Love
2. Love In The Highlands
3. Love Finds The Way
4. The Castle Of Love
5. Love Is Triumphant
6. Stars In The Sky
7. The Ship Of Love
8. A Dangerous Disguise
9. Love Became Theirs
10. Love Drives In
11. Sailing To Love
12. The Star Of Love
13. Music Is The Soul Of Love
14. Love In The East
15. Theirs To Eternity
16. A Paradise On Earth
17. Love Wins In Berlin
18. In Search Of Love
19. Love Rescues Rosanna
20. A Heart In Heaven
21. The House Of Happiness
22. Royalty Defeated By Love
23. The White Witch
24. They Sought Love
25. Love Is The Reason For Living
26. They Found Their Way To Heaven
27. Learning To Love
28. Journey To Happiness
29. A Kiss In The Desert
30. The Heart Of Love
31. The Richness Of Love
32. For Ever And Ever
33. An Unexpected Love
34. Saved By An Angel
35. Touching The Stars
36. Seeking Love
37. Journey To Love
38. The Importance Of Love
39. Love By The Lake
40. A Dream Come True
41. The King Without A Heart
42. The Waters Of Love
43. Danger To The Duke
44. A Perfect Way To Heaven
45. Follow Your Heart
46. In Hiding
47. Rivals For Love
48. A Kiss From The Heart
49. Lovers In London
50. This Way To Heaven
51. A Princess Prays
52. Mine For Ever
53. The Earl's Revenge
54. Love At The Tower
55. Ruled By Love
56. Love Came From Heaven
57. Love And Apollo
58. The Keys Of Love
59. A Castle Of Dreams
60. A Battle Of Brains
61. A Change Of Hearts
62. It Is Love
63. The Triumph Of Love
64. Wanted – A Royal Wife
65. A Kiss Of Love
66. To Heaven With Love
67. Pray For Love
68. The Marquis Is Trapped
69. Hide And Seek For Love
70. Hiding From Love
71. A Teacher Of Love
72. Money Or Love
73. The Revelation Is Love
74. The Tree Of Love
75. The Magnificent Marquis
76. The Castle
77. The Gates Of Paradise
78. A Lucky Star
79. A Heaven On Earth
80. The Healing Hand
81. A Virgin Bride
82. The Trail To Love
83. A Royal Love Match
84. A Steeplechase For Love
85. Love At Last
86. Search For A Wife
87. Secret Love
88. A Miracle Of Love
89. Love And The Clans
90. A Shooting Star
91. The Winning Post Is Love
92. They Touched Heaven
93. The Mountain Of Love
94. The Queen Wins
95. Love And The Gods
96. Joined By Love
97. The Duke Is Deceived
98. A Prayer For Love
99. Love Conquers War
100. A Rose In Jeopardy
101. A Call Of Love
102. A Flight To Heaven
103. She Wanted Love
104. A Heart Finds Love
105. A Sacrifice For Love
106. Love's Dream In Peril
107. Soft, Sweet And Gentle
108. An Archangel Called Ivan
109. A Prisoner In Paris
110. Danger In The Desert
111. Rescued By Love
112. A Road To Romance
113. A Golden Lie
114. A Heart Of Stone
115. The Earl Elopes
116. A Wilder Kind Of Love
117. The Bride Runs Away
118. Beyond The Horizon
119. Crowned By Music
120. Love Solves The Problem
121. Blessing Of The Gods
122. Love By Moonlight
123. Saved By The Duke
124. A Train To Love
125. Wanted – A Bride
126. Double The Love
127. Hiding From The Fortune-Hunters
128. The Marquis Is Deceived
129. The Viscount's Revenge
130. Captured By Love
131. An Ocean Of Love
132. A Beauty Betrayed
133. No Bride, No Wedding
134. A Strange Way To Find Love

A STRANGE WAY
TO FIND LOVE

BARBARA CARTLAND

Barbaracartland.com Ltd

THE BARBARA CARTLAND PINK COLLECTION

Dame Barbara Cartland is still regarded as the most prolific bestselling author in the history of the world.

In her lifetime she was frequently in the Guinness Book of Records for writing more books than any other living author.

Her most amazing literary feat was to double her output from 10 books a year to over 20 books a year when she was 77 to meet the huge demand.

She went on writing continuously at this rate for 20 years and wrote her very last book at the age of 97, thus completing an incredible 400 books between the ages of 77 and 97.

Her publishers finally could not keep up with this phenomenal output, so at her death in 2000 she left behind an amazing 160 unpublished manuscripts, something that no other author has ever achieved.

Barbara's son, Ian McCorquodale, together with his daughter Iona, felt that it was their sacred duty to publish all these titles for Barbara's millions of admirers all over the world who so love her wonderful romances.

So in 2004 they started publishing the 160 brand new Barbara Cartlands as *The Barbara Cartland Pink Collection*, as Barbara's favourite colour was always pink – and yet more pink!

The Barbara Cartland Pink Collection is published monthly exclusively by Barbaracartland.com and the books are numbered in sequence from 1 to 160.

Enjoy receiving a brand new Barbara Cartland book each month by taking out an annual subscription to the Pink Collection, or purchase the books individually.

The Pink Collection is available from the Barbara Cartland website www.barbaracartland.com via mail order and through all good bookshops.

In addition Ian and Iona are proud to announce that The Barbara Cartland Pink Collection is now available in ebook format as from Valentine's Day 2011.

For more information, please contact us at:

Barbaracartland.com Ltd.
Camfield Place
Hatfield
Hertfordshire AL9 6JE
United Kingdom

Telephone: +44 (0)1707 642629
Fax: +44 (0)1707 663041
Email: info@barbaracartland.com

THE LATE DAME BARBARA CARTLAND

Barbara Cartland who sadly died in May 2000 at the age of nearly 99 was the world's most famous romantic novelist who wrote 723 books in her lifetime with worldwide sales of over 1 billion copies and her books were translated into 36 different languages.

As well as romantic novels, she wrote historical biographies, 6 autobiographies, theatrical plays, books of advice on life, love, vitamins and cookery. She also found time to be a political speaker and television and radio personality.

She wrote her first book at the age of 21 and this was called *Jigsaw*. It became an immediate bestseller and sold 100,000 copies in hardback and was translated into 6 different languages. She wrote continuously throughout her life, writing bestsellers for an astonishing 76 years. Her books have always been immensely popular in the United States, where in 1976 her current books were at numbers 1 & 2 in the B. Dalton bestsellers list, a feat never achieved before or since by any author.

Barbara Cartland became a legend in her own lifetime and will be best remembered for her wonderful romantic novels, so loved by her millions of readers throughout the world.

Her books will always be treasured for their moral message, her pure and innocent heroines, her good looking and dashing heroes and above all her belief that the power of love is more important than anything else in everyone's life.

"There is a delightful Beatles' song called 'All you need is love' and, if you think about it, the Beatles are absolutely right!"

Barbara Cartland

CHAPTER ONE
1892

Lady Vanessa Shotworth rose slowly from her chair and walked out of the breakfast room with her head held high, but with a sinking feeling within her.

Once again her stepmother was screaming abuse at her and finding fault in a way that she found humiliating.

Yet there was nothing she could do about it.

She had risen early as it was a lovely sunny day and she had gone to the stables to take her favourite horse for a ride.

Because it was so delightful riding over the fields her father owned and which had belonged to the Shotworth family for five generations, she had forgotten the time.

It was only when she was beginning to feel hot and rather exhausted after galloping for so long did she turn for home.

The birds were singing in the trees and the flowers were brilliant in the garden.

She then walked from the stables where she had left Samson in the charge of the groom and stopped to look at the roses and forget-me-nots that were now fully in flower.

'I am sure that Papa would be thrilled to see them, if he was at home,' she mused.

She was wondering if the flowers in India were as beautiful as they were at his home.

It had been at the request of the General now in charge of his Regiment that he had gone to India for the special celebrations they were making over a battle when they had won a great victory at a time when the English had first taken over India.

As he had always loved his Regiment and had been particularly proud of it, the Earl of Shotworth had gone as requested.

He had told his wife and daughter that he would return home as soon as it was possible.

"I will miss you so much, Papa," Vanessa had said.

He held his daughter close to him as he told her,

"I promise you I will return soon. But you know that the Regiment will plan all sorts of demonstrations for me and I always find it hard to quench their enthusiasm."

"They love you, Papa," Vanessa said. "But I love you too and the house is not the same when you are away."

Her father knew without her putting it into words that she did not get on well with her stepmother.

He had hesitated for quite some years after his wife, Vanessa's mother, had died, simply because he had tried to make his life complete as a widower.

As he was very good-looking, many women would have been willing to marry him for himself and not just his position.

But Cynthia Holman had been not only extremely beautiful but very persistent in her pursuit of him.

She too had been married for a short time. She was a soldier's wife and her husband had been killed in a very small battle, where strangely no one else in the Regiment was even wounded.

The Earl had been Commanding Officer at the time and he had thought it his duty to comfort the wife of a man who had not only been under his command but was a friend.

Having made up her mind that she would marry again and make it a far more prestigious marriage than she had made previously, Cynthia was always at the Earl's side when he least expected it.

She was certainly very lovely in her own way.

And because he too was so lonely without his wife, the Earl found that he was putting a Wedding ring on her finger almost before he had time to think of what his life might be like in the future.

He had already come to appreciate it that he was too old to continue to command the Regiment.

He thought when he retired to his big house in the country that he would undoubtedly be lonely despite the fact that his daughter, Vanessa, was at seventeen about to leave Boarding School and come home to him.

After her beloved mother had died there had been various members of the family she spent the holidays with when her father was with his Regiment.

Although she missed her mother, she longed more than she had ever longed for anything else to be alone with her father at their home in Worcestershire.

It was therefore a shock to her when she learnt that, before he had left India, he had married again and was bringing his new wife home with him.

All her dreams of riding the horses alone with him had been dashed.

And of making him tell her tales of India in the evenings after dinner.

And of increasing the magnificent library which she thought should be brought more up to date.

And above all to have her father loving her as he had done whenever he was on leave from his Regiment and they were together.

'I love him and I know that he loves me and now Mama is dead, I must look after him and make him happy,' she had told herself.

But, when she met her stepmother, she realised that Cynthia clearly had every intention of being not only the most important woman in her husband's life, but she was equally determined to make sure that there was no other around and that included his daughter.

In fact almost from the moment she had arrived at Shotworth Hall, she had done everything to separate the Earl from his daughter.

She absolutely made sure that he concentrated only on her.

What was so infuriating, the new Countess thought to herself, was that her stepdaughter was most undoubtedly a beauty.

That would have been bad enough, but, because it was the complete opposite to her beauty, she hated every golden hair on Vanessa's head and every glint in the blue of her eyes.

Now that the Earl was away in India, the Countess had taken every opportunity of making herself even more unpleasant than she had been previously.

She found fault with everything that Vanessa did.

She criticised her behaviour, the way she spoke and what she said and above all her appearance.

"I suppose you think that you look attractive in that dress," she had said last night when Vanessa came down to dinner. "But personally I think it's in extremely bad taste for a girl of your age and you must have been more stupid than you usually are in buying it."

"Actually it was given to me," Vanessa replied, "by my aunt and, when I wore it at a party she gave, everyone admired it."

"Well, I think it's vulgar and you look overdressed in it," her stepmother snarled.

They sat down in the dining room in silence while the butler and two footmen began to serve the meal.

The Countess had hardly spoken while the servants were present and Vanessa, looking at the empty chair at the head of the table wished, as she had wished a thousand times already, that her father would come back from India.

As she had now entered the house by a side door, she was suddenly aware that, as breakfast was always at nine o'clock, she was late.

Undoubtedly her stepmother would be pleased that it was an excuse for her to be even more disagreeable than usual.

She gave a sigh as she walked along the passage to the breakfast room recognising that her only excuse in not being back before was because she was enjoying her ride so much and it had been an exceptionally fine morning.

She was not mistaken in thinking that, as she was so late, her stepmother would be angry.

The Countess was in the process of pushing aside her plate and rising from the table as Vanessa entered.

"I am so sorry – to be late, Stepmama," she said as she walked into the room. "I forgot the time because it was such a lovely day and the sun was shining so warmly. In point of fact, I could not help thinking that Papa would have enjoyed every moment – if he had been with me."

"But he is not here," her stepmother said sharply. "I have told you a thousand times, if I have told you once, that you are to be on time for meals! It is extremely rude to someone like myself and unfair on the servants."

"As I have told you – I am very sorry," Vanessa stammered. "I completely forgot the time and I apologise."

5

"That is what you have said over and over again. I find it difficult to make you obey even the ordinary rules of a well-run house," her stepmother snapped.

She glared at Vanessa before she went on,

"In fact, as a punishment and perhaps in future it will force you to think more clearly, you are to scrub the kitchen floor this morning. I have already sent a message to the cook to tell her that the scullery maid is not to clean it as she usually does and it is to remain dirty until you do her work as a punishment."

Vanessa stared at her.

"Are you serious in what – you are saying to me?" she asked.

"Very serious, indeed! I have spoken to you again and again about being on time. Perhaps, when you have scrubbed the kitchen floor, you will then find it easier to remember that I run this house and all my orders must be obeyed."

Vanessa stared at her.

"I cannot believe – you mean it," she said. "How could you expect the servants not to laugh when they see me crawling about on the floor and – I will doubtless not clean it half as well as the scullion who does it every day?"

"You will do as I tell you," her stepmother raged. "You will not have your breakfast or any other food until you have obeyed my orders."

Vanessa, who had reached the table while she was speaking but had not yet sat down, stood and stared at her.

"Are you seriously saying," she asked, "that I am to go hungry – because I am a few minutes late?"

"You will indeed go hungry until you have finished the kitchen and if it is not finished in time for the next meal you will miss it too, as you are now going to miss your breakfast."

The Countess glared at Vanessa as she ranted on,

"You have been giving yourself airs and graces for a long time, but you have to learn that I am the Mistress here and, when your father is away, every order I give is to be obeyed and there is to be no argument about it."

"And – if I refuse?" Vanessa questioned in a small voice, almost as if she was talking to herself.

There was silence and then her stepmother sneered,

"Surely you are not deaf as well as being stupid! You will have nothing to eat, and the servants have already been given that order, until the kitchen floor is cleaned."

She paused before she added,

"If anyone dares to disobey me and feeds you, they will instantly be dismissed."

As she spat out the last words, she walked out of the breakfast room and slammed the door behind her.

Vanessa stood staring at the table.

Then she turned to look at the sideboard where she saw that the silver dishes which always held the eggs and bacon for breakfast had been removed.

For a moment she could not really credit that what she had just heard was true.

That her stepmother had really given orders to the servants that she was not to be fed.

'How can she behave so outrageously?' she asked herself. 'It's very obvious that she hates me and resents any affection Papa shows for me. But surely this is going too far?'

At that moment she saw the door of the pantry open slightly.

She knew that Bates, the old butler, who had been at Shotworth Hall ever since her father had first married, was peeping in to see if she was alone.

When he was sure that the Countess was not there, he opened the door wider and came in.

Vanessa gazed forlornly at him.

And then she said in a soft voice just in case her stepmother was listening,

"What am I to do, Bates? What am I to do?"

Bates looked towards the closed door that led into the rest of the house and glanced over his shoulder before he replied,

"If you asks me, my Lady, you should go to stay with one of your relations until his Lordship returns."

"I have thought of that already. But Aunt Alice is not at home, as she is staying with her daughter in Wales, and Cousin Cecily is ill and there are two nurses in the house. I am sure that I would not be welcome there."

"That makes things a lot more difficult," Bates said, scratching the side of his forehead.

"It makes things impossible. My other relations, as you well know, have never been particularly anxious to have me in the holidays when I was at school, so I would feel embarrassed at suggesting that I visit them now."

Bates sighed.

"I'll fetch you something to eat, my Lady, whatever her Ladyship may say."

"No! No!" Vanessa exclaimed. "You must not do that. If you were told to leave because you had disobeyed her orders, it would be disastrous for The Hall. You know that Papa and Mama – have always relied on you."

"That be true," Bates agreed. "But I can't have your Ladyship starving on my hands and cook feels the same."

"Then what I must do is to run away," Vanessa said in a whisper. "And I must be gone before my stepmother has the slightest idea – it's what I intend to do."

Bates nodded.

"That's the sensible thing. But although I've been thinking, I can't imagine where you could go where you'd be welcome."

"It does seem strange, when Papa has done so much for the country – and so many admire him greatly, that I cannot think of anyone close to him who would welcome me," Vanessa replied.

She smiled wistfully as she added,

"And I suppose it's because Papa is so often being consulted by the War Office in London that he had little time for the friends around him even though they came to our ball at Christmas."

"They most certainly did," Bates agreed. "If you asks me, they wouldn't have missed it for anything."

"Of course not, Bates. It was more because balls are few and far between rather than because they wanted to see Papa and Stepmama."

Bates sighed again.

"It be different when your dear mother were alive. Then there were always people coming to the house, bringing her flowers, asking her advice and wanting her to hear their good news as well as the bad."

"I remember that too," Vanessa told him. "If only Mama was still with us, it would be very different."

"Very different indeed, my Lady!" he exclaimed.

"Well, one thing is very obvious," she said. "I am not wanted here and it will be impossible for me to return – until Papa comes back from India."

"His Lordship will want you then, right enough," Bates commented.

Vanessa smiled.

9

"Even though Stepmama hates me – as much as she does, I know that Papa will always love me. But it might be embarrassing if I went out to India to him."

"Your Ladyship couldn't go on that journey alone," Bates said. "It be too far and you'd have to have someone to chaperone you and where could you find one?"

"Where indeed!" she answered. "I cannot think of anyone who would be prepared to take me all that way to Papa. As it takes a long time to reach India, he might easily be coming back while I was going out!"

As it sounded funny, Bates laughed and then said,

"That be true enough, my Lady. So we're back to the same problem. Where can your Ladyship go now?"

"I will think of somewhere, but the sooner I go the better it will be for you all here."

She hesitated for a moment before she went on,

"I know that you would not let me starve, but if Stepmama finds you feeding me, as I know you would, she will make you leave and as I have already said that would be a catastrophe for The Hall."

"But where will you go, my Lady?" Bates asked.

The anxious expression on his face and the way he spoke told Vanessa that he was genuinely worried.

"I am going to go North," she said, "where I am quite sure that I will find friends who have been here and who will find me somewhere to stay and something to do."

"You can't go alone, my Lady," Bates muttered.

"But how can I ask anyone to come with me? You know as well as I do that her Ladyship would forbid any of the staff to come with me."

Vanessa scowled before she said,

"I know only too well, without being told, that her Ladyship wants to humiliate me. And how could she do it more successfully than forcing me to do what the servants do? I would expect that scrubbing the kitchen floor is not the only ordeal she has in mind for me."

"If your Ladyship starts out alone on one of the horses," Bates remarked, "there may be trouble waiting for you outside the main gates."

Vanessa did not answer and he went on,

"I was saying to the Missus just the other night how pretty you looked and that means real danger for a young woman of your Ladyship's age out alone on the road."

"You are not to worry," Vanessa told him. "I am thinking of a cousin of mine who lives in Northumberland, who I am quite certain would be pleased to see me."

She thought for a moment before she continued,

"There is also a good friend of Papa's who lives in Lincolnshire who came to stay almost every Christmas and brought with him quite the prettiest dolls I ever had."

"How do you know he would be alive now?" Bates asked.

"Because he always sends me a card at Christmas," Vanessa replied, "and I received one last Christmas and wrote and thanked him for it."

"Well, I suppose that's where your Ladyship could go if you can't stay here."

"How can I stay here?" Vanessa asked. "I am sure that Stepmama has been thinking out every possible kind of chastisement for me and this may be one of the mildest."

"She be real wicked," Bates replied. "This be your home and his Lordship'll be ever so angry if he comes back and finds your Ladyship's disappeared."

"It's no use, Bates," Vanessa told him quietly, "I have to go. It has been more impossible every day to put up with her finding fault with me."

She sighed before she added,

"I can stand it no longer. Therefore I am going to disappear, not that I think she will make very much effort to find me."

"Well, you're not going through the front door or the back," Bates asserted, "without something to eat."

He smiled at her before he went on,

"If you go into the office, I'll lock the door while you are eating and her Ladyship won't be able to come in. She will only be aware that the secretary has not arrived until tomorrow to give out the wages."

"Then that is where I will hide while you collect the things I want to take with me," Vanessa said.

She walked out of the breakfast room and Bates followed her.

When they then reached the office, she stood up on tiptoe and took the key from the top of the door where it was always hidden.

Bates unlocked the door and Vanessa walked in.

She did not often go to the office, but it looked just the same as it had when she was a child.

There was a great pile of tin boxes that contained, she knew, the history of The Hall and the people who had served her family.

There was also a huge safe where the secretary kept the money for the wages and there were also a number of bookshelves holding the accounts of the household going back for several hundred years.

The desk for the secretary was a large one with an impressive black inkpot in the centre of it.

Vanessa sat down at the desk and a few minutes later Bates came in with her breakfast.

There were eggs and bacon, which was always her father's favourite, along with toast, butter and marmalade and fresh fruit from the garden to finish the meal.

He set down his tray and then went back to shut the door and lock it before he waited on Vanessa.

"To tell the truth, Bates," she said, "I am feeling very hungry. It's all the exercise I have taken. I galloped faster than I have ever galloped before, because it was such a lovely morning."

"Now don't you go exerting yourself on this trip to your friend," Bates told her. "And do stay at a respectable hotel if you can find one and be sure, my Lady, to lock every door of every room you goes into and make sure that no one follows you."

He spoke to her very severely and Vanessa laughed.

"How I wish you were coming with me, Bates," she said. "We would find a good deal to amuse us on the trip."

"I have been thinking, my Lady," he replied, "what you'll be wanting. If you takes money with you, it must be hidden somewhere where anyone curious wouldn't find it."

Vanessa smiled at him.

"You must tell me what I should do and I will do it," she promised, "especially if it assures me coming back here safe and sound when Papa returns."

"Can you image just how his Lordship'd feel if you were lost," Bates answered. "That's why, my Lady, you has to be ever very very careful. You're not to go talking to strange men, however pleasant they may be and you must be very careful where you stays."

He gave a deep sigh before he carried on,

"I've said it before and I'll say it again, you never knows what them inns and hotels, which look ever so nice from the outside, be like inside. If they thinks you've got money on you, it'll be gone by the morning."

"I will be very careful," Vanessa promised. "I know I should not go alone, but it would be impossible to ask any of the household to come with me."

She stopped for a moment.

"As you are very well aware," she continued, "her Ladyship would be furious if she thought that you were feeding me at this moment and helping me to run away."

"I suppose," Bates said, "your Ladyship wouldn't change your mind and stay here if we all help you as much as we dare."

"It will only get you into more trouble than I am in at the moment," Vanessa replied. "But thank you, Bates. You know I rely on you and I will let you know where I am, so that you can tell me if Papa returns unexpectedly."

"I'll be waiting for your letter, my Lady, and I just know the Missus will be praying every night that God will take care of you."

"I am sure He will," Vanessa murmured. "If Mama is in Heaven, which I know she is, she would not want me to stay here and be so unhappy."

"If ever there be a real Lady who everyone loved," Bates said, "it were your Ladyship's mother. A Saint she was before she went to Heaven to become one."

Vanessa smiled as she knew how much everyone had loved her mother.

They certainly had no use for her stepmother, who never went to see any of them in the village and she was completely indifferent to anything that might make them happy or unhappy.

'Why did Papa ever marry Stepmama?' she asked herself, as she had done a thousand times already.

As there was no answer, she realised that the only thing she could do was to keep well away from her until her father came back from India.

She finished her breakfast and, to Bates's delight, she ate not only the eggs and bacon but also all the toast, butter and marmalade.

"Now I ought not to be hungry until dinnertime," Vanessa said. "But, if I am tempted by one of the village inns, I might just pop in to have a mouthful or two."

"Now you be careful of them village inns," Bates warned her again. "Sometimes their looks be a disguise for all sorts of things your Ladyship shouldn't know about. In my opinion the best thing you can do is to ask someone locally where be the best place you can stay the night."

"That is certainly an idea, Bates, but I am sure that in most villages there is only one inn. If any of the houses let out a bedroom, it would be uncomfortable."

"Well, I'll be thinking of that," he answered, "when I knows your own bedroom upstairs be empty tonight and the Missus and I will be worrying ourselves over you."

"You are not to worry too much," Vanessa replied. "I promise, if I'm too frightened or find the going too hard, I will come back."

Bates eyes lit up.

"Does your Ladyship mean that?" he asked.

"I promise you," Vanessa said, "that, if I get into trouble of any sort, I will come straight home."

"I'll remember that," Bates answered, "and I knows that your Ladyship always keeps her word."

"And now, as I am going away, I must have some money," Vanessa said suddenly. "Not too much, but I must be able to pay for my food and my lodgings."

Bates then went over to the safe and Vanessa was not surprised when he took the key from its hiding place and opened the safe where the money was kept.

"I'll inform Mr. Marshall that when you went away you wanted twenty pounds for your trip," Bates said.

"Do you think that will be enough?" she asked. "I would rather have thirty pounds, as I will have to pay for Samson's accommodation too."

Bates very carefully counted out the money and put it on the desk in front of her.

"That be thirty-two pounds. Hide it carefully, my Lady, or it'll be taken away from you before you've got many miles from here."

"Then I would have to come back for some more. I am quite certain that then Stepmama would lock me in my bedroom and perhaps tie me up to the bed!"

She laughed as she spoke, but Bates shook his head as if he thought it a distinct possibility.

She hid the money, which Bates put in a small bag, around her waist and covered it with the blouse she had worn to go riding. The jacket over it was well worn and not smart enough to be noticed.

Bates then went up the backstairs to her room and brought down the things that she knew she would need to run away.

It was impossible for her to go herself because her stepmother believed that she was working in the kitchen.

And it would be suspicious if she was seen leaving her bedroom with anything unusual in her hands.

Bates came back much quicker than she expected and he had with him a light bag she had sometimes carried on Samson, when she had been going to stay the night with a friend in the neighbourhood.

Therefore she would not require a great number of clothes and he had been clever enough to find in her empty bedroom exactly what she wanted.

When she peeped into the bag to see if it was all there, she saw her nightgown and a pretty silk dress that she could wear at dinner and stockings and underwear.

There was also a clean blouse to wear under her riding jacket and a brush and comb, which would not take up too much room.

The only problem was the light shoes she wanted to wear for the evening instead of the riding boots she would wear all day.

Fortunately a part of Samson's harness had been made specially to hold a case on it, if Vanessa wanted to be away for the night and to change her dress and take her nightgown with her.

When Bates came back with her clothes, she said,

"Thank you so much, Bates, for being a dear friend to me. I know that Papa will thank you when he hears how wonderful you have been."

"I've known you, my Lady, since you was a little one, running into the kitchen to show the Missus your new doll," Bates replied. "I never thought the day would come when you'd be turned away from your own home."

"I am going of my own free will," she said. "I know in my heart that this is the right thing to do rather than stay here and fight endlessly with Stepmama."

She noticed that Bates's eyes darkened whenever she spoke of her stepmother.

She thought how wrong it was of her to antagonise the servants when they had been at The Hall for so long and loved her father and mother.

'If ever I have a big house of my own,' Vanessa thought, 'I will make them a friend just as Bates is a friend to me and I will understand their difficulties as he manages to understand mine.'

They left the house by the back door and outside there was a narrow path through the rhododendrons which led to the stables.

Vanessa entered the first stable where there were six horses including Samson, which was her own.

Her father had given him to her four years ago on her seventeenth birthday.

He was indeed a magnificent horse, the largest she had ever had, and he was well-bred and exceedingly swift.

He nuzzled against her and was obviously pleased to be going out again so soon.

"I don't know how far we will have travelled by tonight," Vanessa said, "but don't forget to think about me, Bates. I hope you don't get into trouble when I have left."

"I was just thinking of that," Bates answered. "It struck me that if I instruct James the footman to tell her Ladyship that I've got bad toothache and am resting, she'll not ask me what I was doing when you disappeared."

Vanessa laughed.

"That is clever of you. Of course you must cover your footsteps just as I must cover mine."

They were in Samson's stable and the Head Groom and two others were, Vanessa knew, working in the other stables on the horses and, as soon as they had rubbed them down, they would take them out for a ride.

She therefore hurried to be out of sight before they appeared and she managed it by Bates opening the paddock gate for her.

"Thank you! Thank you!" she whispered to him, so that her voice would not carry. "Pray that I will come back safely as soon as Papa returns home."

"I'll be thinking of you, my Lady, all the time you are away," Bates smiled.

She waved her hand and rode off at a quick gallop.

She knew as she reached the trees and out of sight of the house that she had stolen away without anyone being aware of it.

Now she realised that she had to keep to the fields until she had passed all the cottages in the village.

Then there would be no one to tell her Ladyship in which direction she was going if by any chance there was a hue and a cry after it had been found that she had gone.

She only hoped that Bates would not get into any trouble for having helped her, but she was quite sure that he would be sensible and tell no one where she had gone or what she planned to do.

Once she was away from the village, the sun was shining on the fields she was riding over and the birds were twittering in the bushes.

Because she had, as she well knew, a long way to go, she did not press Samson forward as strongly as she might have done.

At the same time she managed to cover a great deal of ground before it was nearing luncheontime.

'As I had such a good breakfast, I am not really hungry,' Vanessa told herself.

So she gave Samson a drink at the next stream they came to.

Then she pressed on avoiding the main roads, but keeping, where she could, to the fields or back lanes.

It was almost teatime when she felt that they had travelled a long distance and she must begin to concentrate on somewhere to stay the night and to have something to eat both for herself and Samson.

As she was intelligent, she had been aware that she was in sight of the main road almost all the time even though she was not actually on it.

As it happened there was not a great deal of traffic passing up and down.

She thought that, if by some chance her stepmother was looking for her or had sent others to search for her, they would find it impossible to follow her when she went from field to field.

She found that in most fields there was a gate that was easy to pull open and she met no one to accuse her of trespassing.

However, she was now a little tired because it had been so hot and because she had felt, although she did not show it, agitated and full of anxiety in case she did not get away or was stopped by someone pursuing her.

Now that was no longer a menace, but she still had to spend the night somewhere.

It was exceedingly important that it was not the sort of place where, if her stepmother was searching for her, she would make enquiries.

'After all a young woman with a horse is nothing particularly unusual,' Vanessa thought. 'And Samson is a magnificent animal that every man would appreciate. And I am not being conceited when I say that most people think me very pretty.'

She had no idea how lovely she was looking with the sunlight turning her hair to gold.

Her eyes were shining because she was excited at starting this strange and new adventure away from what she had found impossible to bear.

'I know that Papa, when he does return home, will understand,' she told herself many times.

But, although she wanted to avoid it, the nagging questions that kept occurring to her were,

Would she be safe?

Would she reach the North?

Would her friend be ready to welcome her when she appeared unexpectedly?

'I am sure she will,' Vanessa reassured herself.

At the same time the questions were ever present at the back of her mind.

Now she knew that if she was to find somewhere to stay she must ride onto the main road and so risk people noticing her, although, as she then told herself, there was nothing unusual in a young woman riding a big horse.

She paused for a while to pat Samson on his neck.

"You are too good-looking," she told him. "I ought to have chosen one of the dowdy horses to accompany me. Although I cannot prevent it, there is no doubt that you will cause a sensation whenever you appear."

Samson did not answer.

For the first time Vanessa was feeling a little afraid of what lay ahead of her.

After all, wherever she had lived or been while she was growing up, there had always been people to take care of her and to love her. And to make her feel that to them at least she was very precious.

Now she was alone – completely alone.

It then struck her for the first time that, because her father had been in India for so long and because it was what her stepmother wanted, they really had few friends compared to the time she remembered as a child when her mother was in charge of the house.

She was always entertaining her friends who came from London or the country and they found it impossible to pass by without dropping in to see her.

Vanessa could remember them clustering round her pram when she went out with Nanny and she could recall

21

too the many children's parties that her mother had always arranged for her.

But it was her father who was so frequently absent because he was serving in his Regiment.

And when he did come home she felt the tempo rise in the house as her mother was so thrilled and excited.

The servants seemed to move around quicker as if they wanted to please him and many people popped into the house from morning to night merely to have a word with the Earl.

It was indeed very different from how quiet and horrible it had been since she had been left alone with her stepmother.

'If I had been wise, I would have gone out to Papa in India,' she told herself.

Then she knew it was a very long journey that she could not undertake by herself and anyway her stepmother would almost certainly have prevented her from leaving.

'I have done the only thing I could do.' she thought again as she rode towards the village.

She was, however, further away from it than she had thought she was.

She had to cross a field and then there was a wood and then another field before she reached the village itself.

"What you want," Vanessa said aloud to Samson, "is a good evening meal which you shall have whatever it costs and a drink of pure water."

Samson pricked up his ears as she was speaking.

Then she passed through another field, which was, she thought, quite narrow.

At the far end of it there was another wood.

Beyond that would be the village and she hoped somewhere comfortable for the night.

The gate was open and she rode from the field she was in towards the next gate.

It was then she saw that the wood was narrower than she had expected and she could see trees just ahead of her.

Seated underneath the trees with their horses not too far away from them were a number of men.

She thought that they must be working in the field.

Then, as Samson carried her rapidly towards them, she suddenly became aware with a shock that they were highwaymen!

CHAPTER TWO

When Vanessa did reach the highwaymen, she felt that they were looking at her in some surprise.

She realised that they could be very dangerous.

But it was, however, too late to turn round and go back and she had no idea how to get out of the wood.

She therefore drew up beside the highwaymen and sat in the saddle looking at them before she said,

"I wonder if you would be very kind – and tell me if there is a respectable and quiet place in the village where – I can stay the night?"

One of the men laughed and then the others laughed as well.

"Do you know who we are?" a tall man asked.

She thought that he was obviously the leader.

Vanessa was silent and after a moment he said,

"Surely you recognise that we are highwaymen!"

Vanessa looked at him and smiled.

"Are you really?" she asked. "I have always wanted to meet a real highwayman. My father, when he was with his Regiment in India, told me he had two highwaymen in his platoon. He said they rode better than any of the other soldiers."

The man who had been speaking rose to his feet.

"In that case," he said, "I hope you will join us as we are just going to have our evening meal."

"That is very kind of you," Vanessa answered. "I would indeed – like to do so."

She had a feeling that, if she did not agree with them, they might turn nasty and compel her to do so.

She dismounted from Samson and, knowing that he would not stray far from her, she loosened his bridle.

One of the other men rose to his feet and remarked,

"That be a very fine 'orse you be ridin' and one I'd treasure meself."

"He is the one thing I really love and he loves me," Vanessa replied. "I would not part with him – for all the money in the world."

As if he was ignoring what she was saying, the man flung himself onto Samson's back.

He pulled his reins as if he wanted him to ride back into the field that she had just come from.

Just for a moment Samson was still.

Then, as the highwayman kicked him violently to send him forward, he sprung up into the air.

Twisting and kicking the air and behaving as if he had gone mad, Samson finally flung the highwayman onto the ground.

The other men had watched the whole performance with astonishment.

As the highwayman sat up, rubbing the back of his head, Vanessa walked towards Samson.

She patted him and talked to him quietly.

"No one will take you – away from me," she told him. "You are not to be frightened or upset."

The Chief highwaymen then spoke,

"That is the most extraordinary performance I have ever seen. Does your horse often do that?"

"Only when someone tries to take him away from me," Vanessa answered. "A man tried to steal him once and Samson behaved like that. So, bruised and taught a sharp lesson, the man ran away."

"That's a lesson Alfred's learnt now," one of the men sniggered.

"Perhaps, if that is the way you feel about me," Vanessa replied, "I had better go."

"You will do nothing of the sort," the Chief then ordered. "After what you have just told us your father said about highwaymen, we would be interested to hear more about their progress in India."

"My father was in command of his Regiment," she began, "and, when we took over India, he was one of the first to establish control amongst the natives. I think now that it is a very happy country and one I would very much like to visit."

"If your father's in India," one of the highwaymen said, "who's lookin' after you and why are you travellin' alone?"

Vanessa then sat down by him, watching Samson, who, having shaken himself as if to be quite certain that he was free of anyone sitting on his back, was now eating the grass at his feet.

She saw that the highwaymen had in front of them a meal they had obviously bought at one of the villages.

It consisted of large meat sandwiches and slices of currant cake. There were also sausages that one man was heating on a fire further away from the others and she had not seen him at first.

There was beer to drink and bottles of water.

After a moment Vanessa asked shyly,

"Could you spare one bottle of water for Samson? He has come a long way – and I don't like him to drink out of ditches."

"You are quite right," the Chief said. "If there is any rubbish in a field, it is always thrown into a ditch and I have told my men so often that we must find fresher water for our horses than that."

As he was speaking, he poured one of the bottles of water into a bucket.

It was so old that Vanessa thought that they must have picked it up on their way to the field and it did not actually belong to them.

It did, however, hold the water and Samson drank it down to the last drop.

She patted him saying,

"You can have some more later. At least you will not be thirsty for a while."

Then she went back to where she had been sitting and found that someone had put his coat on the ground to make her more comfortable.

She sat down and accepted one of the hot sausages that she found very edible.

It was embarrassing for Vanessa to find that if she wanted a drink she had to drink out of the bottle as there were no glasses.

Because she was thirsty she drank a little water and then wiped the bottle very carefully with her handkerchief before she put it back on the ground.

She was aware as she did so that the highwaymen were watching her all the time.

She was feeling afraid that they might ask her for any money she had on her and, if she refused, they might search her to see if she was telling the truth.

At first the highwaymen ate almost in silence and then the Chief said,

"Now tell us why you are riding alone and where you are going?"

Vanessa drew in her breath.

"I will tell you the truth," she answered him. "I have run away."

This admission interested them all and they raised their heads to stare at her.

"Run away from your home and your father?" the Chief questioned.

"At the present time my father is in India," she told them. "He is no longer serving as a soldier, but, because he was such a success when he was there, they asked him to go back for Regimental celebrations, where I am sure he has received a medal for his many years of Service."

"So you did not go with him?" the Chief asked.

Vanessa shook her head.

"No, I was left behind with my stepmother. As she hates me, she was so cruel and humiliating that I decided to run away."

"Do you know where you are going?" he enquired.

"To the North of England," she replied, "where I have several cousins who I think will be pleased to have me, even though I will be turning up unexpectedly."

"And you are travelling all that way by yourself?" the Chief asked. "It is something you should not be doing, seeing how young you are and what a fine horse you are riding."

"I am aware – of that," Vanessa answered. "At the same time I could not stand being humiliated and insulted by my stepmother any longer. I have been riding all day and only now am frightened because I have to find a place to stay and I am anxious, of course, about Samson."

The way she spoke told the highwaymen listening that she was telling the truth and one or two nodded.

There was silence for a moment and then the Chief suggested,

"Well, I think for tonight at any rate, you should stay under our protection. We will make sure that no one steals Samson or intrudes on you in any way."

Vanessa gave a little cry.

"Will you really do that? Oh, it's kind of you and I am sure that I would feel safer with you than in a strange inn where they might even refuse me because I am alone."

"We are now going to make ourselves comfortable in this wood," the Chief said. "And I promise you no one will interfere with you and no one will steal Samson."

He looked around at his men before he asked,

"Is that agreed?"

"Agreed!" they all responded.

She thought that this must be the way he always led the highwaymen and they both respected and admired him.

"We will have to be careful where we go in the future," the Chief went on, "if we have a lady with us. I think that she will not feel affronted if we ask her for a name that we can use when we talk to her."

Vanessa laughed.

"Of course, we have not yet introduced ourselves, I know it's wrong of me to ask you uncomfortable questions, but I would like you to address me with the name I was christened with, which is 'Vanessa'."

"A very pretty name too," one of the men piped up, "if I ever 'ave a daughter, that's what I'll call 'er."

"Well, now that Vanessa is one of us," the Chief asserted, "we must all protect her for as long as she travels with us."

He paused before he turned to her and added,

"We are going North and I think you would be wise to accept protection from us for as long as it's possible for you to do so."

Vanessa clasped her hands together.

"How kind you are. Now I feel – quite happy about tonight and not afraid as I have been for the last hour or two of being treated suspiciously by some innkeeper who would perhaps refuse – to house me and Samson."

"And you must not forget Samson," the Chief said. "Having seen the way he treated Alfred, I am sure that no one will try to creep away with him in the night or even ride him for that matter!"

There was laughter at this and then Alfred said,

"I've got a pain in me back and I warn all of you boys not to touch that grizzly animal!"

He spoke slowly and the other men laughed at him.

"You were tryin' to be a step ahead of us," one man teased.

Then another chimed in,

"Serves you right! You never knows with 'orses what they'll do next and that's a lesson you'll not forget, Alfred."

Vanessa thought he was being unkind when Alfred had obviously suffered from his fall and she said to him soothingly,

"I hope your back will be better tomorrow and the sooner you lie down and rest it the quicker any damage Samson has done will heal."

"Now you have had your orders, Alfred," the Chief said, "and you would be wise to obey them."

Alfred merely grinned and then the Chief turned again to Vanessa.

"We have chosen this wood because we have been here before," he explained. "There is a cosy little place just behind me where you can cuddle down on your rug, if you have one, and no one will disturb you until we move off early tomorrow morning."

"You are so kind and I am most grateful," Vanessa replied. "Do you think I would be wise to turn Samson loose in this small field? He will not go far as he never leaves me. But I would like to take his harness off him."

"Of course you can," the Chief answered her. "One of us will see that the gates are closed. As I say, we have stayed here before and, as it belongs to an old farmer who we have not yet seen, it's very unlikely that tonight will be the exception to the rule."

"I can only hope so," Vanessa replied, "and thank you again for your courtesy."

They had now finished their meal.

As Vanessa did not want any more to eat, they told her to give the sandwich and the one sausage she had not yet eaten to Samson.

Their own horses were tied up inside the wood, but she saw that the highwaymen had fed them before they sat down for their meal and she respected them for thinking about their horses first.

It was what her father had always taught her to do.

But she knew that a great number of people were much more concerned with themselves than whether their horses were hungry or not.

She took the bridle off Samson's head and then she undid his saddle.

Before she left home, Bates had been wise enough to see that a rug was placed under the saddle and this she knew would cover her while she slept.

Samson was delighted to be free and wandered off, but not too far away.

Vanessa bid goodnight to all the highwaymen, who now were gradually drifting away into the wood.

Finally she was alone with the Chief.

"If you are frightened or feel upset in the night," he suggested, "you are to call to me. I will be quite near you, although you won't see me. It's really quite comfortable here on a summer's night."

"What do you do if it's raining?" she asked.

The Chief smiled.

"That is a question I often have to ask myself," he replied. "We find a shed or some sort of cover to keep the rain out."

Vanessa sighed,

"It is very brave of you to be a highwayman when most people are scared to death of them and the Police are always looking for an excuse to arrest them."

"I am aware of that," he replied. "But unfortunately I was as unhappy at my home as you have been in yours."

He paused for a moment.

"So I took to the road and, because I met these men at some time, they joined me because each of them, if you hear their story, would tell you a very sad one of either neglect, cruelty or worse still, infidelity."

"I have often thought that was the reason why men took to the road," she said. "But, as you know, travellers are very scared of highwaymen. Actually, when I first saw you, I thought that I ought to run away as fast as possible."

The Chief smiled.

"You were brave enough not to do so and I promise you that my men will protect you and treat you with great respect. You cannot ask more, even from a highwayman!"

"Of course not and thank you for being so kind to me. I know that Samson would like to thank you as well."

"You must be extremely careful with that horse," the Chief said. "If I had been advising you to run away, I would not have allowed you to take anything so fine and, of course, so valuable."

"I should have been very unhappy if I had left him behind," Vanessa said. "Although I was apprehensive this evening at what I was doing, but you have been so good to me that I am no longer afraid."

"That is what I want you to say," the Chief replied, "and I think the best thing we can do is to take you as far as we can towards your relatives in the North."

Vanessa did not reply at once and then she said,

"I would like, if it is possible, to thank you for your kindness not only in words."

The Chief drew a little nearer to her.

"Now listen to me," he whispered, "if you have any money on you, you are not to say so in front of the men."

He smiled at her before he went on,

"If they ask you, you say that you ran away in too much of a hurry to think of anything but escaping from the misery you were in."

"I understand and thank you, thank you!"

"Goodnight, my dear," he said. "I just cannot help wishing that we had met in far wiser and perhaps happier circumstances."

He did not say more, but walked into the bushes.

Vanessa gave a sigh and stepped into the hollow in the ground where she had decided to sleep.

She had a last glance into the field at Samson and found that he was lying down, almost like a dog might have done, just a few feet away from her.

It was impossible for her, in these circumstances, to undress.

So she just took off her riding boots and her coat and loosened the front of her blouse which went under it.

She made her coat into a pillow and then lay down on the rug.

Although she had so much to think about, she fell asleep from her extreme tiredness far quicker than it would have been possible normally.

*

She was woken by men talking.

When she opened her eyes, she was aware that she could see the blue sky overhead.

The men talking were the highwaymen saddling up their horses.

Afraid, even after what had been said last night that they might leave her behind, she hurriedly put on her riding boots.

Carrying Samson's harness and saddle, she pushed her way through the other horses to find him.

He was not far away and, when she called him, he came trotting up to her.

She patted him lovingly and talked to him as she saddled him. She had nearly finished when the Chief came through the trees.

"Have you slept well?" he asked.

"I remember lying down and then the next thing I knew it was morning," Vanessa answered him.

"That is just what I hoped," was the reply. "Now we want our breakfast. One of the men has already gone off to fetch it from the inn. He should be back in a minute or two."

Vanessa glanced round to see if they were alone.

Then she said,

"Please, I must pay for my breakfast as indeed you have paid for yours. I am so grateful to you for looking after me and Samson last night."

"Surely even a highwayman is allowed to entertain a friend," the Chief replied. "Just as your father must have fed and clothed those highwaymen with him in India, I am happy to provide you with breakfast if nothing else."

Vanessa smiled.

"It is so kind of you," she said. "I would not have slept quite so peacefully last night if I had been worrying about Samson and you had not been so near to me."

"I have a feeling that you will worry a great deal more about such a magnificent horse before you reach your family. So you must be very careful where you stay."

"Then please may I stay with you as long as I can?" Vanessa asked. "If my stepmother sends for the Police or someone from the estate comes to look for me, I know that they would not expect me to be with highwaymen!"

"They certainly would not," he agreed.

Then he laughed as he added,

"You will find in life, as I have, that it is always the unexpected that occurs. So it is something we appreciate more than we would do otherwise."

"This will most certainly be an intriguing story to tell my grandchildren," Vanessa reflected.

The Chief laughed.

"There are many years for you to enjoy before you have any grandchildren, but they will be most fortunate to have such a courageous grandmother. I do think it's very brave of you to have ridden off by yourself."

"I feel much less worried now than I did the first few hours after I left home," Vanessa admitted. "Thank you again for a delightful night's sleep."

"Well, come along now and have your breakfast," he replied. "It's nearly six o'clock and we should be on our way."

He started to walk to the edge of the wood where Vanessa could see that the other highwaymen were now gathered.

Before they were within earshot she asked,

"Can I stay with you today?"

"We are going North just as you are and I will take you by a route where we will see very few people unless, of course, we have a chance to rob someone."

Vanessa drew in her breath.

While they had been talking so pleasantly, she had forgotten for a moment that the highwaymen were robbers, who were a considerable danger to most travellers.

He began to walk quicker and Vanessa had to hurry to catch him up with Samson following along behind them.

Breakfast from the inn was exactly what she might have expected with eggs and bacon, plenty of sausages and a large pot of coffee.

There were cups without saucers to drink it from and plenty of sugar, which the men stirred into it and drank with relish.

"This be the best breakfast I've 'ad for ten days," one of the men piped up.

"And the most expensive," the Chief pointed out. "You know only too well that our money is getting low and the sooner one of you finds a victim the better."

"There be a main road just ahead of us," one man said, "and plenty of traffic on it. As you know, we need a quiet place to do business and it's no use havin' someone screamin' hysterically after we've gone, which means that they'll alert every Policeman in the neighbourhood."

Vanessa thought that this was common sense, but she did not say so.

Then the Chief said,

"As you say, the main road is ahead. But we have been more successful lately on the minor roads, which lead in the same direction, but which are not frequently used. I suggest that we break up and meet this evening at our usual place which I reckon is about twenty miles from here."

"That's right," one of the men said. "I worked it out yesterday and if you remembers you were lucky on the side road that led us to exactly where we was last year."

"Well then, we should meet there again," the Chief said. "I'll be sorry if any of you come in empty-handed."

"To hear is to obey," one of the men chimed in.

He pulled his mask out of his pocket as he spoke and put it over his eyes.

It was how Vanessa had seen two or three of the men when she had first become aware that they were all highwaymen.

By the time she had ridden towards them they had slipped their masks into their pockets and were looking just like ordinary travellers.

The only difference was that they wore dark clothes and carried pistols at their waists.

As the Chief made no effort to cover his eyes, she felt that she would not be embarrassed at riding beside him.

The men finished their breakfast and, as they did so, each one reached into his pocket and flung down on the ground a few coins that were collected by the man who had brought the breakfast from the inn.

Vanessa noticed that the Chief's contribution was larger than the others and she felt uncomfortable because she guessed that he must have been paying for her.

However, she said nothing as she thought that he would not wish her to do so.

As the six men divided and went off in different directions, two of them waited for the man who had gone to the inn.

Vanessa and the Chief were now finally alone.

"Now, unless you feel you are being followed," he said, "I think we will find it easier riding on the main road. As far as I know the coast will be clear until we reach the place where we are meeting this evening."

"It's very kind of you to look after me," Vanessa replied. "But I will quite understand if you want to be with your men."

"I have a feeling you might have been followed and will therefore have to escape quickly or else you are taken home in disgrace."

The Chief paused before he added,

"Also I have, for the moment, done my work for us all. In fact, to put it briefly, it is their turn to bring in the money and allow us to carry on and enjoy the career we have chosen for ourselves."

"I was wondering last night why you, of all people, would want to be a highwayman," she commented. "After all I recognise from the way you speak that you have been well-educated. So your father and mother could not have been starving when you were born."

The Chief smiled.

"You are very observant," he replied, "and that is a very good thing to be. Yes, I was born in what you might call a very decent community and I went to a well-known school where I eventually became the Head Boy."

"So why, oh why, did you become a highwayman?" Vanessa asked.

"It's a long story and one I have no wish to bore you with," he answered. "But, of course, it was a woman who was at the bottom of it all and I am trying to forget her rather than keep thinking about her."

He sighed.

"All I can tell you is that I suddenly found myself without any money, without a home and there was no one to restrain me or change my luck."

He spoke sharply and after a pause Vanessa said,

"So you took to the road."

"I found it amusing and in a way I was paying back the injuries and unhappiness ordinary people had given me by defrauding them of what they valued much more than anything else. That, of course, is money."

"Do you really make a great deal by stealing?" she enquired.

She thought perhaps that she should not have asked the question, but she could not help being curious.

"Shall I say that I make enough to enjoy myself and to put by a little for when I am too old and have no wish to spend the last years of my life in an Old People's Home or a prison."

"Yes, that might happen," Vanessa said before she could prevent herself.

"I can only pray not and tell you that I am enjoying myself a great deal," he replied. "I do prefer being with men who have suffered as I have in one way or another and who feel they are avenging themselves on the community every time they take money from those people who fancy themselves as being totally superior to anyone as coarse and common as highwaymen."

"But you and I know these things," she answered. "That is why I was so lucky to find you."

"I do like to hear you say that," Chief said, "and I only hope that you will always think of me kindly and, of course, remember me in your prayers."

"I will always," Vanessa promised. "I know, when I tell Papa how kind you have been to me, he will also be very grateful."

The Chief smiled and, as they were at that moment joining the main road that led North, there was quite a lot of traffic.

They rode on the left side of the road in silence and they must have gone about a mile without speaking.

Then the Chief said as if he was thinking aloud,

"You are much too young and too pretty to set off alone in the world. Are you quite sure that these relations you are seeking will welcome you?"

"I hope they will," Vanessa replied. "As they are very impressed by Papa, I feel certain that they will not throw me straight into the gutter even if they don't want to antagonise my stepmother by accepting me."

"Would she dare ask them to do that?" he enquired.

Vanessa sighed.

"I really have no idea what she would do. She is a horrible woman and I know she pursued Papa relentlessly. And it was only because he hated being alone and was so miserable after Mama died that he married her."

She drew in her breath before she continued,

"You have no idea how different she is when she is with him to how she is on her own when she is rude and offensive to the servants. She expresses her hatred for me simply because Papa loves me."

"I know the type of woman you are describing to me exactly," the Chief replied.

Now there was a harshness in his voice that told Vanessa that he too must have suffered.

They rode on until unexpectedly he turned off the main road.

"Where are we going?" Vanessa asked him.

"I think you are feeling hungry and so am I," he answered. "There is a quiet inn where I have been before where the food is good and the publican asks no questions. I think we both deserve a good supper before we meet up with the others to see if they have been successful or not."

Vanessa could not help smiling.

How could she have imagined for one moment that in running away from her dreadful stepmother she would find herself being kindly patronised by a highwayman.

'One day,' she thought to herself, 'I will have to write a book and put in all my adventures. This is certainly one experience that is different from most people's, which will interest and amuse those who read it.'

At the same time it suddenly occurred to her that, if the highwaymen were arrested and she was with them, she might be arrested too.

'Perhaps I should thank them and say goodbye,' she reflected.

Then, because the road they were riding along was empty of other traffic and the fields on either side seemed to stretch away into nothing of any interest, she felt afraid.

'I have no way of defending myself,' she thought, 'if I encountered other highwaymen or even worse still my stepmother has sent the Police after me and I am taken back home in disgrace.'

Without realising it she moved a little closer to the Chief.

41

"Now you are frightened, Vanessa" he said. "What is upsetting you?"

"How do you know I am either of those things?"

"I have learnt, because I have been alone so much, to feel what other people are feeling," he replied. "Also, it is one of the ways in which those who ride with me try to fool me and I know at once. That is the truth, so now give me your answer."

"I was just thinking that it would be frightening if I was with you and you were arrested. Also terrifying if my stepmother has sent the Police – or maybe one of the staff to follow me."

Her voice faltered a little and there was silence for a moment.

Then the Chief said,

"You have to trust me, my dear. I promise you that I will take care of you, just as if you had been my daughter, and I would want neither of the things you have mentioned to frighten her."

"You are so kind," Vanessa murmured. "It was stupid of me not to believe – that you were sent to me from Heaven!"

She hesitated before she went on,

"I thought last night before I went to sleep that my mother was guiding me and – made me join you instead of running off as I would have done in other circumstances."

"I am sure it was your mother who told you that you would be quite safe with me," he said in a low voice. "All I ask is that you trust me and I will save you from being hurt in any way in the future."

"That is a wonderful thing to say," she answered. "If I am to be saved, I want you to be saved too."

The Chief laughed.

"So now you are looking after *me*," he said. "All women are the same. They always think that every man is like a baby they must cradle and prevent from crying!"

"I am afraid that I have cried for too long by myself to worry now whether I am safe or not," Vanessa told him.

"All I think of or try to think of," he said, "is that I must enjoy today as tomorrow might be really different."

Vanessa did not answer.

She was thinking that as he grew older it would be more and more difficult for him not to have a home.

Not to be loved as he must have been before he was so badly hurt and made so utterly miserable that he would do anything so outrageous as to take to the road.

'I wish I could help him,' she told herself.

Then she thought that maybe when her father came home, he would do something for the Chief and make him happy again.

They rode for some time without saying anything and then the Chief said,

"The only thing that matters now is to get you to the North without you incurring any of the unpleasantness that is usually waiting around the corner for pretty young women like yourself who run away."

"Perhaps it was wrong of me," Vanessa said, "but because I was so lucky to meet you, I am happier than I have been ever since my father left for India."

He smiled.

"That is the sort of thing I want to hear," he replied. "At the same time we must, both of us, be very careful."

CHAPTER THREE

They rode on for several more miles.

As it was now late, the Chief turned off the main road and went down a very narrow lane that led eventually to a small village.

"This is where we stay," he said, "when we get as far as here. The people who keep the inn are very kind to me. But I will say, which I think is very sensible from your point of view, that you are my niece."

Vanessa smiled.

"I am delighted to be your niece. I think it is very wise or else they will think it strange for a highwayman to be riding with an elegant lady-friend."

The Chief laughed.

"That is exactly what I was thinking. As you know, people are always curious and want to know more than the person concerned wishes to tell them."

"That is true enough. I found at school that the new girls were always asked endless questions the moment they arrived. Then a little later they wished that they had not said so much."

They rode on through the village and then at the far end there was a very small and unimpressive inn. It was obviously very old as it was all in black and white.

But Vanessa realised from the rough bench outside and its many diamond-paned windows, most of which were broken, that the publican was not a wealthy man.

He was in fact old with a long white beard and he greeted the Chief with delight.

So did his wife who was grey-haired and wearing spectacles.

"We were wonderin' what'd 'appened to you," the publican said, "and prayed that it was no worse than you'd want to tell us."

"No, it's all perfect as far as I am concerned," the Chief told him, "and I have brought you my niece, who is on her way to stay with some of her relations in the North."

"Then we're ever so glad to 'ave 'er," the woman said, "and we'll make 'er as comfortable as we can. But you know we're always hopin' for some money which'll give us the chance to do a bit of decoratin'."

"I think everything is fine the way it is," the Chief replied, "and I am really looking forward to one of your delicious dinners. I have told my niece that you ought to be cooking for the Nobility rather than us!"

They all laughed and then the publican's wife said,

"You shall 'ave the best I can get in an 'urry, but don't expect miracles."

Vanessa was then shown into a small and narrow bedroom upstairs, which was badly in need of paint on the walls and the carpet had many holes in it.

But the place was spotlessly clean and the sheets had obviously recently been washed.

When they put Samson into the rather dilapidated stable on the other side of the inn, she had been relieved to find that the food for him was good and the water fresh.

She gave him a hug before she went back into the inn and thought that she was lucky not to have to sleep next to him under a hedge or, as she had last night, in a wood.

When she had washed and put on the pretty gown she had with her that Samson had carried on his back, she

45

thought that it was a pity she was not going where anyone could see her and admire her gown.

Then she told herself again that she was very lucky.

If the highwaymen had been bad men, they might have taken everything from her, including her money and Samson, in which case she would have had to walk home in ignominy.

She sent up a little prayer of gratitude to God that she had been saved from not falling into the hands of really desperate highwaymen.

She arranged her hair so that it looked very pretty and put just a little rouge on her cheeks.

Then she went downstairs to find that the Chief was sitting in the bar talking to the publican.

Apparently there were no other customers at the inn that night and even the bench outside was empty.

The Chief rose from his seat when she joined them and said in admiration,

"You look so very smart, Vanessa, that I ought to be taking you to the Ritz instead of giving the birds and the ducks something to talk about!"

He laughed as he added,

"But at least I can drink your health and I will ask the publican, who you realise is an old friend, if he will let us have a glass of champagne."

"That sounds extravagant to me," Vanessa sighed. "Equally I am delighted to be able to drink your health."

"And I want to drink yours," he replied, "because I worry about you wandering around by yourself without a chaperone of any kind and without anyone to protect you from dangerous men like myself."

His eyes were twinkling as he spoke and Vanessa laughed.

"No one could have been kinder," she said, "and I drink your health with all sincerity and hope that you will always be happy."

"That is just what we all hope for, but unfortunately things don't always go the way we want them to."

It was late in the evening when they had had what Vanessa thought was a really delicious but simple supper and they were watching the moon climbing up the sky.

It was then she asked and she thought it very brave of her,

"Do tell me why you became a highwayman? I am sure that you were not born to be one. It seems such an odd choice."

He looked at her and quizzed,

"Are you really interested or just curious?"

"I am greatly interested," she answered, "because you have been so kind to me. If I could do anything to help you, you know I would only be too glad to do so."

She spoke with such sincerity that he reached out, took her hand in his and raised it to his lips.

"If I was a young man again," he said, "I would be inspired to great things to please you. But, as I am getting old and will soon have to retire, I will now answer your question by telling you the truth."

He checked himself for a moment before he said,

"That I feel is in some ways the best compliment I can pay you."

"So you mean that you have not confided in many people?" Vanessa asked him.

"No, of course not. The men I work with are all running away like you and have their own problems, the most important being to keep themselves out of prison."

"I rather fancied that was the reason men became highwaymen," she answered. "But tell me why you did."

For a moment he was silent and she thought that perhaps she had asked too much.

Then he said,

"I belong to quite a decent family. My father was a Bank Manager although not a particularly senior one, but he was respected by everyone in the town where we lived."

Vanessa sipped the glass of wine she had brought from the dinner table and then she moved a little closer to him so that she would not miss a word of his story.

"Because I was very energetic and found the small town we lived in had little to offer me, I joined a well-known Regiment."

He smiled at her before he continued,

"Because I was young and keen and, if I may say so, a particularly good rider, I soon rose in the Officers' eyes. And eventually, after we had been abroad, I became a Corporal and a year later a Sergeant."

Vanessa wanted to ask what countries he had been to, but thought it unnecessary to interrupt him.

He only paused for a while before he went on,

"It was abroad that I did especially well, which I enjoyed more than being in England where we had little to do except parades at various times of the day."

Vanessa did not say anything.

"I am sure that the Officers would not admit it," he told her, "but we had far too much time on our hands with nothing to do."

He smiled.

"It was inevitable that the younger men should get into mischief. Actually I was then a Sergeant when I met a very pretty young woman who was more intelligent than the average woman we soldiers go out with."

He spoke as if he was looking back into the past and Vanessa was now finding his story fascinating and was listening to every word.

"There was this one woman in particular" he went on, "who was, I thought, very attractive. She was anxious to open a bookshop in the village where books could also be borrowed at two pence by anyone who was capable of reading them."

He took a deep breath before he added,

"I helped her and then unfortunately I was sent off with a small company of men to take part in some parades in a large town nearby."

Vanessa was watching intently.

"There were celebrations," he told her, "which I do not remember much about, but we stayed under canvas in the vicinity for nearly a week. When I came back, I found that my friend was being pestered by a man who I can only describe as a vagabond, but who thought that any woman he fancied was fair game."

He sighed as he continued,

"Because my friend was frightened of him and then I found her struggling in his arms, I knocked him down. When he attempted to fight me, I knocked him down again and gave him a little of what he deserved."

"In other words," Vanessa said, "you rendered him unconscious."

"Unconscious for a brief moment," he agreed, "but quite conscious enough to drag himself bleeding and with a broken arm to the first Officer he found and complained bitterly about my treatment of him."

"So what happened to you then?" she asked almost breathlessly.

"I was brought in front of a panel of Officers who, on these occasions, behave like Police more than soldiers."

"And what happened to you?" she asked again.

"Eventually, after listening to a great number of lies told by my opponent, I had to be confined to barracks for two weeks in what was actually solitary confinement. To put it bluntly, it was imprisonment."

"Surely that was very unfair?" Vanessa gasped.

"That is what I thought at the time and I resented it very much. So much so that, when I was finally freed, I resigned from the Army and went abroad."

"How did you manage to do so?" Vanessa asked.

"My family gave me a certain amount of money to travel simply because they were shocked and ashamed by my behaviour. In fact they said that I had not only ruined my reputation but theirs. As you can well understand, the story unfortunately got into the newspapers."

"Oh, no!" Vanessa exclaimed.

"Well, news was short and it was the type of thing they enjoyed while my father, as Head of the Bank, was horrified and disgusted that any son of his should have fought in what he reckoned was a common ruffian way."

"But you were fighting for the honour of your lady-friend," Vanessa commented.

The Chief smiled rather bitterly.

"She as well had no use for me after I had been branded by the local newspapers as well as my family."

"But you were really fighting for her," Vanessa said again, almost as if she was speaking to herself.

"That is what I thought," he replied, "but of course, it was not anything people could see or understand, while the man with a broken arm and a battered face received all the sympathy."

"So what did you do?" Vanessa enquired.

"As I told you, I went abroad," he replied. "I did not wish to make my family more bitter than they already were and my father coldly gave me a little money, which meant that he was rid of me."

"How could they be so unkind?" she questioned. "After all you were only fighting a man who was behaving disgracefully to your friend."

"That is what I thought and what I still believe, but I enjoyed going abroad even though, having no money, I had to take on the most menial jobs on a ship to go there and to do even worse tasks when I arrived as long as I was paid for them."

"So what happened then?" Vanessa asked.

"Well, after a year or so I found that I had enough money to return home, if I wished to," he told her. "I had, in one way or another, travelled a great deal and seen much more of the world than most men of my age."

"But you still wanted to go home?" Vanessa said enquiringly.

"I wanted to because however pleasant foreigners might be, we not only don't talk the same language but do not have the same ideas or thoughts as they have,"

"I can understand," Vanessa murmured.

"When I arrived back in England," he continued, "I was getting on for forty years of age. Despite everything I had gained, or thought I had, I still had an empty pocket."

"But surely your family were ready to help you?"

"I had been away for nearly ten years," he told her. "My father had retired and had, I learnt, almost forgotten I existed, although he still remembered what he called 'the blot' I had made on the family name."

"So what did you do?" Vanessa murmured.

"I found that my family did not want me and so I thought, having seen so many other countries, I would see some of England."

He paused for a moment before he commented,

"To be honest with you, because I had very little to spend, I stole a horse, which was in a field outside the town where the main part of my family lived."

Vanessa stared at him.

"I then rode away on it," he went on, "meaning to discover the amusements and delights of my own country, of which actually, I knew very little."

Vanessa was listening intently as he continued,

"It was then, quite by accident, I met, when I was finding a place in a wood to stay the night, a highwayman. He had just robbed an old woman of her handbag which she had left in her carriage while she was leaving flowers at a nearby Church."

He glanced at her as he went on,

"He did it so cleverly, he told me, that none of the servants driving the open carriage had been aware of his thieving. He showed me with much glee that the handbag contained a large sum of money, both in silver and gold."

"He must have been very lucky not to be caught."

"That is what he thought and so did I at the time. But, because we struck up a strange friendship that night, he insisted that I went with him the next day and watched him gather what he called 'juicy fruit' from people who were too careless with what they possessed."

"It must have been interesting for you, even if you were taking no part in it," Vanessa said.

"I found it fascinating," he admitted.

He smiled at Vanessa and resumed his tale,

"I could hardly believe my eyes when we met again in a wood where we had slept the previous night that he had managed to collect over thirty pounds in small coins, three pretty handbags, two umbrellas and a cape he told me he would be able to sell for at least another ten pounds."

"It sounds unbelievable!" Vanessa exclaimed.

"That is what I thought at the time, but it intrigued me that anyone could be so clever or that the people who owned the goods could be so careless."

"So you thought you would do the same."

"Not at once," he replied. "My friend who enjoyed being with me because he claimed that he often felt lonely showed me how he held up a carriage wearing a black mask, which he told me he always carried in his pocket."

He hesitated before he carried on,

"He would get away with quite a considerable sum of money while the gun he pointed at the servants on the box kept them looking right ahead as he ordered them to."

Vanessa gave an exclamation.

"It all sounds too easy to be true!"

"That is what I thought at the time, but I soon learnt that people when confronted by a highwayman with a gun are too frightened to make a fuss about handing over what he requires. And once you have ridden away they have no chance of catching you up or denouncing you."

He stopped talking for a moment and then added,

"In fact I think they are too ashamed as a rule to tell anyone what has happened to them."

Vanessa gave a sigh.

"So you took to the road permanently."

"To tell you the truth, it amused me," the Chief replied. "It kept me busy and it kept me rich enough to enjoy good food like we enjoyed this evening and as much wine as I could pay for."

There was a poignant silence before Vanessa asked,

"But surely you are very lonely?"

"I was at first because my friend who taught me so much preferred working on his own," he answered. "Then gradually I met other men who were just as much alone as I was. They not only enjoyed talking to me but found it a new game at which we inevitably won."

He smiled as he added,

"It gave me a new excitement that I had certainly not experienced at other times of my life."

"I suppose you mean the danger," Vanessa said.

"Of course it was very dangerous. Once or twice I thought that the Police would win and I would end up in prison which I assure you is something I wished to avoid at all costs. At the same time every man, whether he likes it or not, finds it a thrill when he does something dangerous and gets away with it."

Vanessa could not think of anything to say.

While she was thinking over what the Chief had told her, he too was thinking.

Then he said,

"Now that I am fifty-five I have made up my mind that enough is enough."

"You mean you are going to give it up?" she asked.

He nodded.

"Yes, I mean to settle down in some special place overseas and make friends."

"What about the friends you have?" Vanessa asked. "Those who have been riding with you and who you are meeting in two or three days' time?"

He smiled.

"They are all young and enthusiastic. I just hope that they will keep out of the hands of the Police until they too are old enough to retire."

"You don't think that they are doing anything that is wrong?" Vanessa questioned.

She thought perhaps it was a personal question and something that she should not have asked, but he replied,

"I have instructed them often enough not to injure anyone. Also never to steal money from anyone who is obviously too poor to part with it."

He paused before he went on,

"They concentrate on the owners of smart carriages and women wearing plenty of jewellery. Also on men who have drunk too much because they can afford it, who will never miss the odd few pounds they have taken from them when they stagger away from some drinking tavern."

Vanessa gave a laugh.

"You make it seem as if you should be commended for doing such good work, just like Robin Hood!"

"We only take from the rich what they can afford and give to the poor who really need it," he replied. "I can swear that no one has really suffered losing anything they could not afford, but have only lost a little of what they have in plenty."

Vanessa laughed again.

"You are now justifying yourself in every possible way," she said, "and it's very smart of you."

"That is what I thought myself," he answered. "It has kept me very interested and provided me with plenty of intelligent young men to talk to. You would be surprised if you knew the background of some of those who have been with me for a short while and then felt inspired to go back to morality and doubtless settle down to be a respectable gentleman in their old age."

"Is that what you have chosen for yourself?"

He sighed.

"I hope so. I know you are thinking that I would be wise to stop before I am caught and I do agree with you."

"Then do give it up," Vanessa implored him. "If I was your wife or your mother, I would always be terrified that one uncertain step might land you in prison and you know how much you would hate that."

"Of course I would," he agreed. "But so far I have been lucky and may I say even luckier in meeting you."

Vanessa smiled at him.

"You have been so good to me," she said. "I might have fallen into the hands of someone who would have taken away everything I possessed and just left me crying by the roadside."

"That is what I am afraid of if I let you go on by yourself," he replied. "Therefore I intend to take you to your family even if to reach there safely I have to behave with propriety so as not to leave you alone."

"You are so kind," Vanessa answered, "and I am most grateful. I realise now it was crazy of me to run away alone and ride all the way to the North. What would have been terrible is that I could have lost Samson."

"That is just what Alfred was thinking of when he tried to ride him. And Samson's behaviour saved me from telling him that he could not rob someone I was offering our hospitality to."

"I knew you would feel like that," Vanessa replied. "If I had lost Samson, I would lose the only friend I have."

She hesitated before she went on,

"That is why I could not leave home without him."

"We have ridden quite a long way today," he said, "and tomorrow we will be nearer your relations. But we must still have quite a good way to travel."

Vanessa knew that he was warning her that they might come into difficulties and so she said quickly,

"I am more grateful than I can say to you, but, of course, I don't want to interfere or alter your life in any way. If my being here makes it dangerous for you, you must tell me to ride away as rapidly as I can."

"I thought you would understand," he said. "Now, my dear, I think it is time for us both to go to bed as we have a long way to go to where we will be meeting up with the others."

He paused before he went on,

"We must leave early. In fact I am going to ask the publican if we can have breakfast at six o'clock."

"Then I must retire to bed at once," Vanessa said. "But first will you come with me to see that Samson has been fed and I always like to say goodnight to him."

"Just as I say goodnight to my horse," he replied. "We will go together and tell them that they are lucky to have owners who make a fuss of them and who consider them even more important than a human friend!"

Vanessa laughed and then she said,

"When I talk to Samson, I am quite certain that he understands far more than if I was talking to a girl of my own age."

"I am sure that my horse, who incidentally is called 'King', is far more interested in what I tell him than what he learns from other horses that he undoubtedly despises!"

It was the sort of remark that would have amused her father and she thought that she must remember to tell him when he returned from India.

Vanessa and the Chief then went to the stables at the back of the inn.

She kissed Samson goodnight and told him that she loved him.

She was aware that the Chief was patting his horse and talking to him in the same way that her father always talked to his horses and he treated them as life-long friends not animals.

When they walked back into the inn, the Chief said,

"Now go to bed. I will thank the publican and his wife for taking care of you and you are to sleep peacefully and not to worry about anything until I knock on your door tomorrow morning at five-thirty."

"You said we were leaving at six o'clock," she said.

"Yes. You have to be dressed and breakfast will be downstairs for you at a quarter-to-six," he replied.

Vanessa chuckled.

"Now you are talking to me like a recruit in your Regiment, who, like me, has no idea of what might happen to him next."

"You are quite right. Therefore quick march up the stairs and my orders are to blow out the candle in exactly five minutes!"

She ran up the stairs aware that he was watching her until she reached the top.

She turned round and waved her hand to him and he waved back. Then she hurried into her room in order to carry out his orders.

Inside her very small bedroom she undressed and then she knelt to say her prayers.

She felt sure that it was her mother who had led her so cleverly to the kind highwayman and he was protecting her from being frightened as she would have been had she been travelling alone.

"Thank you! Thank you so much, Mama!" she said. "Please, please help this nice kind man not to be lonely and unhappy when he gives up being a menace on the roads and then has no one to talk to."

She could understand him finding it rather fun to be with the strange collection of young me he 'worked' with, as he called it.

When she thought about them, she was sure that one or two were highwaymen just for the devil of it.

Others, she then ruminated, must have suffered an injustice or bereavement at home that had driven them onto the road.

Perhaps one at least was like herself escaping from something that was really horrible and degrading and being happy because he had other highwaymen to talk to and was no longer alone.

'It will be difficult after this,' she thought, 'ever to think of highwaymen as being cruel and treacherous.'

She fell asleep almost as soon as her head touched the pillow.

*

She awoke with a start and realised that it must be five-thirty in the morning.

She had obviously slept through the night without waking once.

She dressed quickly, hiding her money in her waist, as she had done on the previous days.

Then, having put her nightgown and her brush and comb back into the saddlebag that Samson carried, she ran down the stairs for breakfast.

The Chief was already there.

He rose when she came rushing into the room and smiled at her.

"Punctual to the minute," he said. "Full marks and I promise you a special medal at the end of the journey if you continue to do so well!"

"I will keep you to that," Vanessa grinned.

It was a hot breakfast of bacon and eggs with some superb coffee.

When they had finished, they thanked the publican of the inn and his wife.

"Now you take extra good care of yourself, dearie," the woman said, "and come and see us when you returns back South."

"I most certainly will," Vanessa promised. "Thank you for a comfortable night's rest and the very delicious food."

"I felt you'd enjoy what I gave you for breakfast," the woman said. "You won't feel 'ungry for a few hours 'owever fast you 'as to ride."

The publican gave them his good wishes and saw them off as they rode their horses from the yard.

"What nice people," Vanessa remarked when they were out on the road.

"I have always found them good friends," the Chief replied. "Although I think that they are suspicious of what I do, they never refer to it."

"What makes you think that they know?" Vanessa enquired.

"Well, I am usually accompanied when I stay here by one or two of the men I work with. Although I have warned them to be careful of what they say, it is something they usually forget. I have seen the publican listening to them with a question in his eyes if not on his lips."

Vanessa smiled.

"Surely they don't think that I am one of the gang since I am a woman?" she asked.

"No. That is why I was anxious that they should see you. I think, although I cannot be sure, that they have completely altered their opinion of me."

"So I have been a little useful at any rate," Vanessa laughed.

"Very useful, indeed," he replied. "Now we have a great deal of ground to cover so we really must hurry or the others will be waiting impatiently for us and maybe getting into trouble because we have not arrived."

"As I am so sure that should not happen," Vanessa answered, "I am prepared to make Samson stretch his legs and I can assure you that your horse will have to struggle to keep up with him."

"I can well believe it. Now let's turn our heads to the North and ride as quickly as we are able to do."

They set off at a brisk pace.

There was no doubt that while the Chief's horse was an exceptionally fine one, Samson was the faster.

In fact Vanessa had to pull him in a little so that she should not get too far ahead and lose him.

She could not help thinking again and again how lucky she had been to find someone who was so generous.

She was almost a little disappointed when, after a short time spent in getting something to eat for luncheon, they arrived at the place the Chief had been aiming for.

It was, strangely enough, the ruins of a very ancient Church that had been abandoned a hundred years ago.

Now there were only ruins with a few gravestones jutting out of the grass that had grown up all around them.

It was most certainly not the sort of place that the average person would visit and it was not surprising that was why it had been chosen by the Chief.

They arrived there at four o'clock in the afternoon and Vanessa saw that he was disappointed not to find any of his men waiting for him.

They had, however, only just dismounted and were looking for a stream to water their horses.

The Chief said that there was one at the end of the field on the other side of the ruins.

Then suddenly they saw two men come galloping towards them.

They waited until the men reached them and had dismounted hastily from their horses.

"I was beginning to think that you were going to be late," the Chief said to the man nearest to him.

In a breathless tone the man replied,

"They've got Alfred! He did somethin' very stupid and, as the Police seized 'im, we only just got away in time!"

CHAPTER FOUR

For a moment the Chief stiffened and then he asked in a restrained voice,

"What has happened?"

"Alfred argued with the woman whose bag 'e was tryin' to take from 'er carriage," the man replied. "That allowed the coachman to signal for a Policeman. 'E came up and arrested Alfred almost afore 'e was aware what was goin' on."

The highwayman stopped to catch his breath before rattling on,

"We moved away as quick as we could, but we saw the Policeman puttin' 'andcuffs on Alfred's wrists. Then another Policeman came runnin' up the road towards us."

He paused again.

"We then slipped away," he went on, "and I don't believe they realised we was with 'im. At the same time Alfred is such a talker I wouldn't be surprised if 'e doesn't tell 'em who we are and where we are meetin'."

The highwayman spoke a little hysterically and for a moment the Chief did not reply and then he said,

"We must, of course, disband as we always have done and meet again later."

"I just thought you'd say that," the other man said. "But I bet Alfred talks about you and bein' with a lady's so unusual that you'd better 'ide yourself quick."

"I am aware of that," the Chief answered bitterly.

Then the man went on,

"You know 'ow 'e 'ated bein' thrown by that lady's 'orse and I bet you 'e tells the Police that 'er be with us."

Vanessa looked at the Chief before she said,

"I must, of course, go on alone."

"Wait a minute!" he ordered. "Let me fix these two men and then I will see to you."

He turned towards the two men and said,

"What I want you to do is to ride East. Don't do anything on the way, but just escape from here. I will go West and that will be something, if Alfred talks, they will not expect."

"Yes, of course, you be right," one man replied.

While the other suggested,

"The sooner we starts off the better."

"Exactly!" Chief agreed. "We will meet in three weeks or a month's time at our usual place. If I am late, don't wait for me, because I may be too far away to come back to you quickly."

"We'll try," the other man said sharply. "But now we must be away. I never did trust Alfred! As far as I'm concerned, they can keep 'im in prison for a year or two!"

He jumped back on his horse and moved farther down the road.

Vanessa was sure that there would be a lane leading off the main road that would take them East.

The two men were in such a hurry to leave that they did not even say goodbye and the Chief watched them until they were out of sight.

Then he said quietly,

"Now we can think about ourselves or rather I must think of you, Vanessa."

"I suppose I will have to leave you," she said sadly. "If Alfred has informed them about us, they will be looking for a man and a young woman on two fine horses."

She was aware as she spoke that the Chief's horse was nearly as spectacular as Samson.

It would be a stupid Policeman who passed them by and was not aware that they were the people they were looking for.

"There are some trees to shelter in at the end of this field," the Chief told her, "and there we cannot be seen from the main road, although I doubt if the Police, however quickly they arrive, will catch up with the two men who have just left us."

He did not wait for Vanessa to answer, but mounted his horse and rode down the field with her behind him.

There was a small copse at the end of it and beyond it there was a lane and beyond that a river.

The Chief stopped under the trees and said,

"Now listen to me, Vanessa. I was thinking only last night of something you might do, but I was reluctant, as you will understand, to give up the delight I found in our companionship. I can only wish that I did not have to lose you."

"It would be dangerous for you not to, but I will miss you terribly," Vanessa replied.

He smiled at her and then he said,

"I will miss you too. But, as you well know, my sort of life is not the sort your father would choose for you under any circumstances, although he would think I was right in guarding you as far as this."

"He would be so grateful to you," Vanessa replied, "as I am. But I do understand that I must go on alone."

"That is something you are not to do," he insisted.

Vanessa stared at him.

"What do you mean by that? You know I cannot go back to my home. Please don't tell me to do so."

"I have not even thought of sending you back," the Chief answered. "But about a mile away from here there is a huge Castle belonging to the Marquis of Westfield whose protection would now be exactly what you need."

"I don't understand what you mean," Vanessa said.

"Well, let's get off our horses and sit comfortably under the trees," he suggested.

He smiled at her as he continued,

"I am certain that the Police will not look for us here and if, as we all suspect, Alfred has indeed talked and talked, they will be riding as fast as they can to find two magnificent horses ridden by you and me."

"They must not find you," Vanessa asserted.

"Not if I can help it, but now listen to me because this is important to you."

"I am listening," Vanessa told him.

Because she was frightened, she slipped her right hand into his.

He held it in both of his.

"It's a local joke," he said, "although it's one that the Marquis does not appreciate in the least, that he cannot keep a Governess for more than a week or so."

Vanessa stared at him, but she did not interrupt.

"The publican, where we stayed last night, told me that Governesses have been rolling in and out of Westfield Castle as if they were fish in the sea!"

"But why?" Vanessa asked, "I don't understand."

"I actually knew the Marquis several years ago," he said, "and found him a clever young man in those days.

But he had not yet come into his title and estate and was very popular among men of his own age."

"Then what happened?" Vanessa asked.

"He was the second son and so not very likely to inherit. He was determined to enjoy himself without, as he called it, 'any restrictions'."

"So what happened then?" Vanessa asked again.

"His elder brother and his wife were drowned in a storm at sea," he replied.

"How terrible!" she exclaimed.

"It was certainly terrible for them and worse still for their daughter."

"So they had a daughter," Vanessa said almost to herself.

"She is now twelve years old and it's impossible for her uncle to do anything with her. She refuses to do anything he tells her and no Governess will stay for long!"

Vanessa laughed as if she could not help it.

"It's not funny for the Marquis, I assure you," the Chief told her.

"I can appreciate that," Vanessa said. "At the same time it does seem ridiculous that a child of twelve should cause such a commotion that everyone is talking about it."

"They always talk and gossip about someone who lives in what they call 'the Big House'," he answered. "It is a famous Castle and I would very much like to visit it myself. So you can easily see that anything that happens there is watched, talked about and, of course, exaggerated by the locals."

There was silence before Vanessa asked him,

"I suppose you are suggesting that I offer myself as a new Governess."

"I was told last night that they were looking for one and finding it very difficult. In fact I was thinking perhaps it would be wise for you to stay there only for a short time, simply because I realise that people would talk if they saw you amongst a band of highwaymen."

"You have been so kind to me," Vanessa answered, "and I don't wish to lose you."

"I have no wish to lose you either," he answered, "but I have to think of what your father would do in such a situation and I am certain that he would think, as Alfred has been arrested, that we must all disappear completely and it is hard to make Samson look anything but a winner."

Vanessa laughed.

"He would be delighted at the compliment."

She was looking so pretty when she laughed that he thought it would be impossible for any man, Policeman or not, to pass her by on the road and not be curious as to who she was and what she was doing.

"What I suggest," he said quietly, "is that you apply for the position of Governess. Then in two weeks' time or a little longer if possible, you set off again to your relations in the North."

He smiled at her.

"No one will think for a moment," he continued, "that being a Governess you could associate with anything so low as a highwayman!"

Vanessa grinned.

"You make it sound very grand. But you know as well as I do that you are not just an ordinary highwayman. When Papa comes home, you have to promise that you will come to meet him. I know he will be delighted to see you. As you say you knew him once years ago, he will want to hear all everything that you have done since."

"Just as I will want him to tell me all the things he has done. But you have to promise me, Vanessa, that you will give me time to get away. Also to make the Marquis as well as other people sure that you have not had anything to do with anyone so lowly as a highwayman."

Vanessa did not laugh as he expected her to do.

Instead she said,

"I will miss you so much. It has been wonderful riding beside you and seeing a different world from the one I have known before."

"At your age and with your good looks," he replied, "there are many different worlds for you to sample. Each one will, I know, welcome you with open arms."

"I only hope that you are right, but, if the Marquis's niece does drive me away as quickly as the others, he can hardly be annoyed when it is something that has happened a dozen times before."

"I am sure he is immune to it by now and be certain that he pays you for the time you have stayed there before you leave," the Chief said this with a twinkle in his eyes.

Then Vanessa answered,

"It has been such fun being with you that I have no wish to teach a tiresome little girl. You know as well as I do that Governesses in most houses are very lonely as they are not grand enough to be with the people who employ them, but too grand to be with the servants."

He chuckled.

"I am sure that is true. But you need not stand it for long. Anyway it is doubtful from all I hear if you will last two weeks at the most."

"Perhaps I will be an exception to all the rules," Vanessa answered. "I expect the child has her own story to tell if anyone will listen to it."

"Well, that is what you must do. I promise you now that we will meet again even if I have to wait until the newspapers let me know that your father has come home covered with glory and, of course, has been received at Windsor Castle."

"I only hope that will be the truth. It would please Papa and everyone tells me that he has done wonders in India."

"I feel sure that he has and now, my dear, I must be on my way, but I suggest that you should stay here in the sunshine for at least twenty minutes."

He smiled at her.

"Then you can proceed," he carried on, "not along the main road where, of course, they will be looking for you, but along these narrow lanes that I am sure will reach the Marquis's grounds, which I think are around half a mile from here."

There was silence and then Vanessa said,

"I will do as you say because I know it's the right thing for us not to be seen together and I could not bear anything to happen to you."

"Someone once said I had a charmed life," he said, "and that is what I believe. Therefore, goodbye, my dear, take very good care of yourself and promise me that you will not do anything silly, but just wait patiently until your father returns and then you must go home."

"Yes, of course," Vanessa replied. "But I expect it will be a long time before he does so."

"As he is so important, the newspapers will tell you what has happened to him," the Chief said, "and I am quite sure that the Marquis will take the newspapers."

The way he said it made Vanessa laugh and, as he helped her to stand up, he declared,

"I hope one day before I am too old I will have a daughter like you. So you can put that in your prayers, which I am quite sure are always answered."

"They were certainly answered when I found you," Vanessa replied. "I was just beginning to be frightened after running away and was so terrified that my stepmother might find me."

She paused before she went on,

"You have been really wonderful and made me feel that somehow I will be able to stay away and be safe from her and from anyone else who might hurt me."

"That is exactly what will happen," he assured her, "and now we must say goodbye."

He bent down and kissed her cheek as her father might have done.

Then, before she could say anything more, he had mounted his horse and started to move out of the wood.

She watched him until he reached the road and then he turned round in the saddle and waved to her.

Vanessa waved back.

She watched him until he was out of sight and then she sat down again on the ground.

'This has certainly been an adventure,' she thought, 'and one day I know that Papa will be interested to find out exactly what has happened to me.'

She said a little prayer that none of the highwaymen would be caught and that even Alfred would not get too long a sentence from the Magistrates.

Samson was quite happy to stay among the trees eating the fresh grass.

Because she felt that she must do exactly what the Chief had told her, she sat there for over half-an-hour.

Then she mounted Samson and, moving slowly into the lane, she began to ride along it, knowing that, as there was no one in sight, she would be unseen.

She must have ridden for a mile before she realised that the land on either side of her was richer and better cultivated than the land she had left behind.

She realised then that she must be on the Marquis's estate.

Ten minutes later she could see the chimneys and the roof of what was obviously a very large Castle.

As she drew nearer, she saw a standard flying from the centre of the roof, which meant that its owner, in this case the Marquis, was at home.

Nearer still she was aware that The Castle was very large indeed, in fact, most impressive and even beautiful with the sun shining on a profusion of windows.

When she had a first sight of the garden, she knew that it was as colourful and almost as beautiful as her own garden at home.

She drew in Samson and kept him still for a while as she gazed at the different colours of the flowers.

There was a smooth green lawn and in the centre of it a magnificent and, she thought, a very ancient fountain.

'It's just the sort of garden I have been trying for at home,' she thought. 'It has obviously been improved over the centuries and it will be a long time before I catch up with it.'

Then resolutely telling herself that there was no need to be intimidated, she turned towards the front door.

Even before she could dismount, a footman in a smart uniform appeared at the door.

When she did not dismount, he ran down the steps to ask,

"Can I help you, miss?"

"I understand that this is the house belonging to the Marquis of Westfield," Vanessa said. "I was told to ask for his secretary who I understand is looking for a Governess."

The footman smiled.

"That's right, miss," he answered.

There was a twinkle in his eyes which told her all too well that the Governess was a joke.

Then she said,

"As I was passing this way, I thought, before I went further North, that I might apply for the position."

"I'm sure his Lordship'll be glad for you to do so, miss," the footman replied and there was a distinct note of amusement in his voice.

"Shall I go to the stables to leave my horse there?" she asked.

"No, I'll take him," the footman answered, patting Samson as he spoke.

Then he added,

"A very fine horse you has here, if I may say so."

"He likes you to say so," Vanessa said. "After you have put him in a stable, I would be grateful if you could see that he is given some fresh water to drink."

"You leave that to me, miss," the footman replied. "I can see he's a fine horse and I'm sure His Lordship'll want to see him."

Vanessa slid off Samson's back and then patted him before she walked to the front door.

As she did so, the footman led Samson away and was talking to him in a manner that told her he had not exaggerated when he said that he was used to horses.

By the time she had walked up the steps there was another footman waiting just inside.

"I think I have to ask for the secretary," Vanessa said, "as I understand that his Lordship is advertising for a Governess."

Vanessa was aware that it was with difficulty that the footman did not laugh.

But he was too well trained and he merely said,

"If you'll come this way, miss, I'll tell Mr. Wilson that you're here."

She followed him along a corridor, which was as impressive as The Castle had been from the outside.

There were paintings on the walls which she knew were priceless and inlaid furniture that she was sure was generations old.

At the end of the corridor the footman stopped and knocked on a door.

When a voice called out "come in!" he opened it.

"An applicant for the position of Governess, Mr. Wilson," he announced.

An elderly man, who was sitting at a desk writing, looked up in anticipation.

When he saw Vanessa, he rose to his feet.

"This is a surprise," he smiled, "but you are very welcome."

Vanessa shook his hand and he indicated a chair in front of his desk.

She sat down and he said,

"It is kind of you to come here, but the Agency did not tell us that you were on the way."

"I did not come from the Agency," Vanessa replied. "I was told in the village, as I was riding North, that his

Lordship required a Governess and, although I was going North for a holiday, I thought that I would apply for the position."

Before the secretary could reply, there was the ring of a bell on his desk and he rose to his feet.

"His Lordship wants me now," he said. "Will you excuse me while I tell him that you are here and perhaps you would be kind enough to give me your name?"

Vanessa had been prepared for this and she knew that it would be a mistake to give her real name or for that matter her title.

Instead she said demurely,

"My name is Vanessa Dawson."

The secretary smiled and hurried from the room.

Vanessa looked around her and then realised that the room was well furnished.

Besides the official books that filled one bookcase, in another there were a number of books appertaining to the history of the Marquis's family.

'I hope that they will take me for at least for two weeks,' she said to herself. 'Then I will have a chance to see all the treasures that the Marquis has here.'

She was so interested as she walked towards the bookcase and saw that she was right in thinking that there was not only the history of The Castle but the history of the Westfield family.

'I will try to stay here,' she thought, 'if only to enjoy the inside of this magnificent Castle.'

She wondered if she dare take out one of the books to read and then she thought that it was not the sort of thing that a well-trained Governess would do.

It was lucky that she had controlled herself because a moment later the door opened and Mr. Wilson appeared.

"His Lordship is in this afternoon," he said, "and he would like to see you, Miss Dawson."

Vanessa smiled at him.

"I do hope I get the job," she said, "because then I can ask you if I could read some of these exciting-looking books. I am certain that the history of the family must be very interesting as I understand that they have been here for many generations."

"They have indeed," Mr. Wilson replied, "and, of course, if you stay I will be delighted to help you choose the most informative of these books."

Vanessa felt he almost said,

' – if you stay long enough!'

Instead he led the way along a corridor to what she thought must be the centre of the huge house.

He then opened a door when they had gone some distance and, because she was staring at the paintings as she passed them, she almost fell over him.

"Here we are," he said, "and I hope you will stay with us at least for a little while."

"I hope so too," Vanessa answered.

He opened the door wider and she walked in.

She saw at once that it was the Marquis's study when she saw a large writing table in front of the window.

It was one of the most impressive-looking rooms she had ever seen and there were magnificent paintings of horses and dogs on the walls.

A huge glass-fronted bookcase was at one end of the room and there were French windows opening into the garden.

She saw armchairs and a sofa covered in dark blue leather that somehow gave the room a somewhat masculine touch which otherwise might not have been noticeable.

Standing by the window was a tall man.

When he turned round, he was, she felt, very much younger than she had expected him to be.

The Chief had told her that the Marquis's brother and his wife had been drowned and that was why he had come into the title.

She had thought that he would be getting on for forty, but the young man facing her was at least ten years younger. She was to learn later that he was twenty-seven.

As he walked towards her holding out his hand, he said in a deep rather attractive voice,

"How do you do, Miss Dawson. I understand from my secretary that you are here applying for the position of Governess to my niece."

"I was told that you were looking for one, my Lord," Vanessa replied. "And, as I am on my way North, I thought that it was perhaps an opportunity that I should not miss."

The Marquis smiled.

"I think it was wise of you. Equally I am not going to pretend, as I expect you have been told, that it is not an easy position."

"I was told you have employed quite a number of Governesses," she replied. "I thought, although I might be wrong, that someone younger than a Governess usually is might be more successful."

"I did not think of that," the Marquis then admitted. "Sit down and tell me about yourself. Surely you are not travelling entirely alone?"

"Actually I was not travelling far," Vanessa told him. "As I expect you will have heard, my Lord, that I am riding a very fine horse which is a quick mover. Therefore it was far easier to be alone than to be accompanied by someone who could not keep up with me."

The Marquis laughed and replied,

"I have often felt like that myself and found it very annoying to keep having to pull my horse in rather than encourage him to go faster."

He motioned to her to sit down in an armchair and then he said,

"I expect you have been told that my niece, who lost her parents at sea a year ago, is not an easy pupil."

Vanessa did not reply and he went on,

"Of course the people round here have little else to talk about. They have made the most of the fact that I have found it difficult to keep a Governess for long as my niece unfortunately takes a dislike to them almost as soon as she sees them."

"I suppose we have all felt like that about teachers at one time or another," Vanessa remarked.

"Of course we have," the Marquis replied. "I well remember one tutor I had in the holidays, who I disliked violently from the moment he arrived until the moment he left. But then my parents were extremely annoyed with me rather than with him."

"But at least you do understand the difficulties of a teacher," Vanessa replied, "when they have to please a child rather than argue the point with someone older."

"All I know," the Marquis said, "is that Melinda, for that is my niece, has very strong views on education and is determined, if possible to learn nothing."

He sighed before he added,

"I find that very difficult to cope with."

"I am not surprised," Vanessa agreed. "But if you give me a chance, my Lord, perhaps I may succeed where others have failed."

There was silence and then the Marquis said,

"You really look too young to be a Governess."

"I assure you," Vanessa retorted, "I will be a very good one. I was Head of my school before I left and, because my father is a very intelligent man, I learnt a great deal from him. In fact more than most women acquire in a lifetime."

The Marquis stared at her and then he remarked,

"That is the best reference I have ever heard anyone give of someone else, let alone themselves."

"I am sorry if I sound conceited, my Lord. It just happens to be the truth, because, as I was not expecting this to happen, I have nothing with me in writing."

"What I would like to say," the Marquis replied, "is give us a chance. If you fail, you fail, and I have no idea what I can say to you to make it sound easier, but you have to take things as they are and make the best of the situation, if it's at all possible."

Vanessa realised from the way he spoke that things were very bad.

His niece had obviously been determined to be rid of every new Governess whatever she was like or however qualified she might be.

There was silence until the Marquis said,

"I would be most grateful to you for attempting to teach my niece even the most ordinary things. In fact what I feel she really needs is companionship of some sort."

He paused before he went on,

"I have tried to find girls of her age locally, but no one around here wants to join in with what after a day or two invariably becomes a disaster."

Vanessa smiled.

"All I can promise your Lordship is that I will do my best. If I fail, I will continue on my journey."

There was a twist to the Marquis's lips as he said,

"I suppose I should really ask you a great many questions about yourself, but to be honest it's a waste of time. I can only say that I think it is very brave of you to undertake the position and I do hope that you will succeed where a great many others have failed."

"I will certainly do my best, my Lord. All I ask is that, if at first I seem somewhat unconventional, I am only doing what I feel may be successful in the long run."

The Marquis stretched out his hands.

"Have it your own way, Miss Dawson," he replied, "and I will not interfere. As you may realise already, I am merely begging for your help."

"And I am begging for you to give me a chance," Vanessa replied with a smile.

She hesitated for a moment before she said,

"One thing you might think very strange is that I have no luggage with me. I was riding to the North and my luggage went ahead in the usual way, while I preferred to ride with as little as possible."

"I think you are very brave," the Marquis remarked, "to travel alone. Rather than send unnecessarily for your clothes, my housekeeper could dress a dozen people from the stores that have accumulated during every generation."

"It sounds fascinating, my Lord, you must not be surprised if I come down dressed as Mary Queen of Scots or perhaps someone from several centuries earlier!"

The Marquis laughed and then he said,

"I can tell you one thing, Miss Dawson, you are quite different from every Governess I have interviewed. I have a distinct feeling that, where everyone else has failed, you will succeed."

"It's always a big mistake to count your chickens before they are hatched," Vanessa warned. "But I will do my best and if I fail I hope you will be kind enough to at least let me stay here for tonight."

The Marquis threw up his hands.

"Tonight and for a thousand nights if you can do it for me," he replied.

"I think that is asking too much," she answered. "But can I now meet your niece, my Lord?"

The Marquis was silent for a moment.

She guessed that perhaps the child had refused to meet prospective Governesses in the past.

"What I suggest," she said, "is that you send me or take me up to the nursery or schoolroom wherever she is and let me meet her alone. I am sure it would be a mistake for you to introduce me as the new Governess."

"Perhaps you are right and it is something that we should not have done in the past," the Marquis agreed. "I can therefore only wish you all the luck in the world which incidentally will be my luck too."

"Miracles do happen when – we least expect them," Vanessa replied.

"Very well then," he said. "I will now take you up to the second floor where my nursery was when I was just Melinda's age, which now is used as a schoolroom."

Vanessa wanted to say that this was a mistake from the beginning, but she thought that she must not criticise until she was quite sure that she was on firm ground.

As the Marquis then walked towards the door, she followed him. They went into the passage and she saw just a little further on that there was a magnificent staircase.

It was, she thought, just the kind of staircase that one descended in an elaborate gown aware that one was being admired from below as one did so.

Or alternatively, when one was younger, one slid down the banister far more swiftly if not so elegantly.

'This is certainly a very fine Castle,' she thought, 'and I must see it all before I am forced to leave which I will undoubtedly be.'

Then, as the Marquis started to walk slowly up the stairs, she followed behind him.

She was thinking that The Castle itself was a story to fill hundreds of books.

If the people in it were, she thought, as original and unusual as The Castle, then this was not only a background for a book that she would like to write but certainly a good hiding place from her stepmother.

Because she had been so happy with the Chief, she had not thought about her very much except when she went to bed at night.

But now she was determined that she would stay here if she possibly could and not return to the woman who treated her so badly in her beloved father's absence.

The horrendous stepmother, who not only made her miserable but was determined to humiliate her in front of the servants.

'I will stay,' she thought as they reached the second floor.

Then, as the Marquis stopped outside a door, she knew that this was the battleground where she must win or leave The Castle which she so wanted to explore.

As far as she was concerned, it was the one Castle that would always fill her dreams.

'I must stay! *I must*!' she told herself.

As the Marquis stood outside the closed door and looked enquiringly at her, she suggested,

"Please let me go in alone. I will come back and tell you later whether I am to stay or ride away defeated."

The Marquis grinned at her and then he said in a low voice that was little more than a whisper,

"Good luck! If you succeed I will be more grateful that I can possibly express in words."

"I should think it is a question of neck and neck," she said.

The Marquis's eyes twinkled.

"If I have a choice," he said, "I would bet on you. But as it is, I can only hope that by some miracle you are a winner."

'It is what I have always intended to be,' Vanessa thought.

Then she remembered vividly how she had had to run away from her dreadful stepmother.

But because she did not wish to appear afraid, she held her head high.

"Wish me – luck, my Lord," she said.

Opening the door before the Marquis could do so, she walked into the room.

CHAPTER FIVE

For a moment she thought that the room must be empty.

She went in and closed the door.

It was then she saw, hidden by an armchair, that there was a young girl sitting on the floor and playing with some coloured bricks.

One quick look at her told Vanessa that she was exceedingly pretty.

Her golden hair cascading onto her shoulders was naturally curly.

As the girl looked up to see who had come into the room, Vanessa put her finger to her lips to indicate silence.

Then she walked across the room in the opposite direction to where the girl was sitting and opened a door to see where it led.

She closed it again and turned towards another door that actually was a wardrobe.

And that too she closed.

Still without speaking and moving on tiptoe, she walked nearer to the girl and then asked in a whisper,

"Is anyone listening?"

Melinda was watching her with surprise.

Now, having been asked the question, she hesitated before she replied,

"No! I don't think so."

Vanessa looked over her shoulder again as if she wanted to be quite certain.

Then she knelt down on the floor beside the girl and very quietly asked,

"Will you help me?"

"Help you!" Melinda exclaimed in an astonished voice. "How can I do that?"

Vanessa looked over her shoulder again as if she was still afraid that someone would overhear what she was saying.

Then she went on,

"I am here at The Castle in disguise and pretending to be a Governess."

"Pretending to be a Governess!" Melinda cried out. "But I don't want a Governess."

Her voice became louder as she went on,

"I won't learn! I won't!"

Vanessa gave a deep sigh.

"But I want you to help me. I thought you would do so."

"So how can I help you?" Melinda enquired.

Vanessa looked over her shoulder again.

"I am not a Governess and I have run away," she whispered.

Melinda's eyes widened.

"Run away, but how?"

"My stepmother was so very cruel to me," Vanessa began. "My father is away in India and she said that she would starve me if I did not do what she wanted."

Melinda was now obviously interested.

"What did she ask you to do?" she enquired.

Vanessa, still speaking in just a whisper, replied to Melinda,

"She said I had to clean the kitchen floor in front of the servants. If I did not do so, she would starve me and give me no food until I obeyed her."

Melinda, who had obviously been very well treated by her uncle, listened in surprise before she said,

"That was very wrong and very cruel of her."

"I thought you would understand," Vanessa replied. "So I have run away to find somewhere to hide, so please, please hide me. I am so frightened I will be taken back by a servant who will be sent to look for me. It will not be difficult to find me because I am riding a very big and marvellous horse."

Melinda sat down more comfortably on the ground.

"Do tell me exactly what has happened," she asked. "I don't understand."

Vanessa looked over her shoulder again before she said,

"I told your uncle that I am a very experienced Governess, so he has employed me. If I can stay here for a little while, perhaps my stepmother will give up searching for me. Oh please, Melinda, please help me!"

"I want to help you," Melinda answered, "but just suppose she finds you?"

"If you hide me in one of the cupboards or perhaps in the cellars, she will go away or rather whoever she has sent to find me will go away because, and this is a real secret, I have not given my real name."

"That was clever of you," Melinda said. "So who do they think you are?"

"They think – at least your uncle does – that I am a real Governess and my name is Miss Dawson."

"And you did not tell him about your stepmother?" Melinda questioned.

"No! Of course not!" Vanessa replied. "I just said that I was looking for a job and, as I knew that he was advertising for a Governess, I came to offer my services here."

Again she looked around the room as if she was frightened.

Then Melinda commented,

"I am sure that no one will find you here if you have given a false name."

"But as I have told you," Vanessa answered. "I am not a Governess. Therefore we will have to pretend that we are doing lessons."

Melinda stiffened.

"How can we do that?" she asked.

"I was thinking how we could do it when your uncle brought me up the stairs," Vanessa replied, "and it's quite easy."

"So how can it be easy to pretend to do lessons?" Melinda questioned. "I won't do *real* ones."

Vanessa was silent as if she was thinking.

Then she said,

"You have so many lovely paintings here and you could show me one of a King or Queen in history. Then I will tell you about them."

She waved her hands as she added,

"And that will be a history lesson."

Melinda laughed.

"Is that all?" she asked.

"Well, we will have to invent all sorts of different ways for all our 'pretend lessons'," Vanessa replied. "For instance, we would be telling the truth if I persuaded you to count the horses in the stables."

She smiled at the child as she went on,

"Then if there were, say twenty, and I asked you how many legs they all had and you said 'eighty', then that would be an arithmetic lesson."

The girl laughed as if she could not help it.

"Do you think that they will believe us?"

"We have to make them believe us, otherwise I will be sent away and may have to go back to my stepmother. She is so horrid and unkind to me that I just want to cry."

"You cannot do that!" Melinda exclaimed. "In fact you must stay here and we will tell everyone that you are teaching me very well."

"Oh, you are so kind!" Vanessa cried gratefully. "I was afraid you would say 'no' and I would be caught and taken back in disgrace."

"I promise I will hide you," Melinda replied, "and as The Castle is so very big, they will never be able to find you."

"Of course not and thank you, thank you, Melinda, for being so understanding!"

Again she looked over her shoulder before she said,

"No one must know that we are playing a game and I think the first thing you should do is to show me as much of The Castle as you can, so I will know exactly where to run and hide if I see my stepmother coming and cannot find you."

She paused before she went on,

"And you must come down to the stables and see my marvellous horse. He is the only one who really loves me now that my Papa is abroad. And we will have to hide him too if people come searching The Castle for me."

"I am certain we will be able to do that," Melinda answered. "I would like to see your horse and also show you mine."

"That is what I want more than anything else," Vanessa told her. "It's a lovely day, so perhaps we can go riding and you can show me a hiding place in the woods where I can go if my stepmother's men should try to find me and search the house."

"I think Uncle Edward would stop them from doing that," Melinda pointed out.

"He might be glad to be rid of me if he does not think I am teaching you the proper way."

"I will not let him send you away," Melinda said sharply.

"If you are helping me," Vanessa replied, "he must not know that I am not who he thinks I am and that you are hiding me. We must just pretend that we are doing things normally. Then he will not suspect if they come looking for someone who is behaving badly that it's me."

Melinda put her head on one side.

"I see what you are trying to say," she replied, "and I do understand that we have to deceive everyone."

"But the most important person to deceive is your uncle," Vanessa said. "Otherwise, if he sends me away, I will have to go at once."

There was silence for a moment and then Melinda said,

"I sent the other Governesses away because they tried to make me do lessons. I have decided not to do them because they are so dull."

"Our 'pretend' lessons will be great fun," Vanessa promised. "But you must not laugh too much because, if anyone is listening, they will think it odd."

"I don't care what they think," Melinda retorted. "They bullied me and bullied me to make me do lessons with cross-looking women who I hated from the moment I saw them."

She pouted as she added,

"I would much rather be alone than be pestered into learning a lot of rubbish just to please them."

She spoke in an angry way that Vanessa knew had upset her uncle.

She therefore suggested,

"Then let's laugh and be happy. That is what I want and I am sure it's what you want too."

"Of course I do," Melinda agreed. "But I have no chance of being happy now that Mama and Papa are dead. Uncle Edward only talks about my education, so I do *not* want to be educated."

"I don't blame you," Vanessa answered. "I suggest that we tell the truth by saying that we are having lessons, which will be jokey ones between you and me."

She laughed as she added,

"At the same time we will enjoy having horses to ride and lots of things to explore."

Melinda put her head on one side.

"What is there to explore," she questioned.

"You would be surprised at what you could find on a big estate like this," Vanessa told her. "Do you know that once Papa and I found a thrush's nest with four tiny birds that had just hatched out of their shells?"

She saw that the girl was interested and went on,

"Another time we found four tiny rabbits that had just been born and we took them home and made them comfortable. I fed them all every day until they were big enough to run off on their own."

90

"I want to do that," Melinda cried enthusiastically. "I call that very exciting."

"There are always exciting things when you have a wood and I have found very thrilling things in the garden," Vanessa told her. "What really is fun, but you must not tell your uncle in case he forbids it, is to climb up a tree and then watch the people underneath it, who have no idea that you are there."

Melinda laughed.

"I should enjoy that especially if Uncle Edward was with one of those pretty women who come here to try to capture him and make him marry them."

"How do you know that?" Vanessa enquired.

"Because the servants talk about it and I heard them saying that the last lady, who stayed here a week ago, was determined to take him up the aisle and he was just as determined not to go."

Vanessa chuckled.

"I can understand that happening. Men who have a title, like your uncle, are always pursued by women who want to be important. And the only way they can manage it, as they are too stupid to use their brains, is to marry a man with a title."

There was silence and then Melinda said,

"I don't want to marry a man just because he has a title."

"Then it shows you have a lot of brains," Vanessa remarked. "But you also want brains to see that a man does not marry you simply because you are pretty and the niece of your uncle, who has a very high-ranking title."

Melinda looked thoughtful.

Then she said,

"Do you think men might want to marry me for that?"

"Why not?" Vanessa asked. "It would make them feel significant to say 'my wife is the niece of the Marquis of Westfield'."

"I did not think of that before. I just thought of Uncle Edward being pursued by these women."

"When you grow up, you will be pursued not only because of that but because you are very pretty and very intelligent," Vanessa replied.

She paused before she continued,

"It's so essential for a woman these days to have a brain otherwise she gets pushed about and men think that they can do anything they like with her because she is not strong enough to have her own opinions on anything that really matters."

Again there was silence while Melinda thought this over and then, as if she was rather frightened by the idea, she said,

"Suppose we go and look at the stables and do what you said was to be my arithmetic lesson."

Vanessa laughed.

"Yes, let's do that," she agreed. "I want to show you Samson and I am sure that you will admire him. He is very clever and always understands everything I say when I talk to him."

"You talk to your horse!" Melinda asked in some surprise.

"Of course I do," Vanessa answered. "My father told me when I was small that it was essential for my horse to recognise my voice and understand what I was saying to him. When you meet Samson, you will see that he listens to me and I am certain that he understands every word I say."

"So let's go and see him now," Melinda suggested excitedly. "I have never thought of talking to the horse I am riding."

"Well, you try it," Vanessa told her, "and I am sure that you will soon find that he is listening to every word you say just as a dog will prick up his ears when you talk to him."

"I had a dog of my own once," Melinda replied, "but I had to leave him at home when I came here because they thought, as he was a mongrel, that he was not smart enough to be with Uncle Edward's grand dogs."

The way she spoke told Vanessa that she had been most upset at leaving her dog behind.

She made a mental note that the girl should have a dog of her own as soon as possible.

'They should have coaxed her instead of trying to bully her into doing what was right,' she thought.

Melinda, who had risen to her feet, ran to the end of the room to open a door that Vanessa thought must lead into her bedroom.

She had no shoes on her feet and Vanessa guessed this was something else that she was rebelling against.

However, she did not say anything, but just waited until Melinda appeared wearing shoes on her stockinged feet.

"If we go down the backstairs," she said, "no one will see us. I expect, if Uncle Edward saw me, he would give me a lecture on how I must attend to my lessons."

"You must not tell him what our lessons are going to be like," Vanessa said in a whisper.

"Of course not" Melinda promised, "I would never do that. But let's avoid Uncle Edward and go to the stables the quick way."

"I am ready," Vanessa replied. "As you can see, I am wearing riding clothes because I have been riding every day since I ran away and actually have no other clothes with me."

"Then we will have to find you some," Melinda said.

"It would be very kind of you. I can hardly walk around in this riding habit every day and I only have one dress, which I slipped into a bag on Samson's back. But I would be bored and so would you be, if I had to wear it day after day."

"I am sure Mrs. Shepherd, who is the housekeeper, will be able to find you something," Melinda answered. "She is not half as bossy and unpleasant as the other maids, who tell me all the time that I have to be a good little girl as if I had a Nanny to look after me."

"Forget that they are difficult," Vanessa said, "and let's enjoy ourselves. There are too many difficult people in the world and I have always thought too few horses like Samson."

Melinda laughed at this.

Then, opening the door, she looked up and down the corridor before she beckoned,

"Come on! We will go the quick way to the stables and no one will see us."

Vanessa followed her thinking that at least she had won the opening round.

She felt certain that little Melinda would be happy with her as long as no one interfered.

As The Castle was a big house, they saw no one as they walked down various backstairs, along corridors and finally they found an obviously seldom used door into the garden at the back.

Melinda was leading the way.

She opened the door, put her head out and said,

"There is no one about. Come on! Quickly!"

Vanessa followed her.

The long twisting path between the large bushes of rhododendrons brought them out on what was clearly the main path to the stables.

Vanessa could now see the angled roofs a little way ahead of them.

With a faint smile she wondered if the Marquis was waiting for her to come down the stairs and say, as she was sure a number of other Governesses had said, that Melinda was absolutely hopeless and that she had refused to speak to them however hard they had tried.

When they reached the stables, Vanessa led the way to where she thought that Samson would have been put.

She was not mistaken.

As soon as the door opened, Vanessa saw the horse she loved just in front of her in a very comfortable stall.

"So here he is!" she said triumphantly to Melinda. "Now let me introduce you to what I believe is the most wonderful horse in the world."

Melinda grinned.

Vanessa entered the stall, knowing, as she did so, that there was good food in the manger and fresh water in a bucket on the ground.

Samson was obviously pleased to see her and, when she talked to him and put her arms round his neck, he then responded by rubbing his head against her.

"Now listen to me, Samson," Vanessa said. "This young lady is very anxious to meet you and I want you to be very nice to her."

She smiled at Melinda.

"She is most unfortunate," Vanessa continued, "as she does not have a marvellous horse like you to love her and you know, if we go riding every day, that she will have to have one who is as quick and spirited as you."

She was certain, as she was talking, that Samson was nodding his head.

When he rubbed his nose against her, Melinda was obviously impressed.

"I can see you have everything you want," Vanessa said, "but if there is anything else, you must ask me and I will understand and then I can tell them what you require."

"Will he really be able to tell you?" Melinda asked.

"Yes, of course, Samson will tell me. Not in words, but, as I have talked to him so much and he has listened to me, we understand each other."

She knew as she spoke that Melinda thought that this was indeed a good idea.

Then she suggested,

"Now show me your horses and tell me the one you like more than the others."

"Come into the next stall," Melinda replied.

Vanessa put her arms round Samson's neck again and hugged him.

"She will never find anyone quite as clever and as wonderful as you," she said, "so you have to be very kind to whoever she takes out riding so that they will try to be as gracious and as fast as you are."

"Uncle Edward is supposed to have the best horses in the whole County," Melinda replied, as if she was a little piqued by what Vanessa had just claimed.

"I will bet you sixpence that they are not as fast as Samson," Vanessa said. "We will race tomorrow morning, but show me your horse now and I will see if Samson will be jealous or perhaps merely conceited because he is so much better than yours."

Melinda laughed and then led the way to another stall.

There were a number of horses in it and Vanessa knew at a glance that they were exceptionally fine.

It was what she had expected. But she was also prepared to be disappointed knowing that people always boasted about their horses in no uncertain terms.

Then she found that compared to Samson they had really nothing to boast about.

But here there was most undoubtedly a fine choice of horses and she asked Melinda as she assessed them,

"Which one is your favourite?"

"They told me that I have to ride a pony," Melinda grumbled. "Although I told Uncle Edward I had ridden a horse as big as Papa's, he still insisted that I had to ride a slow pony, so I said that I would not ride at all."

"But you must ride," Vanessa answered. "I think it is very important for you to be able to control one of these beautiful horses."

"They are Uncle Edward's and I don't think that he will let me ride one of them," Melinda answered. "He is frightened they might run away with me, although I want to run away myself."

"Do you really want to do that when you have such a collection of superb horses to talk to, to look at and, of course, to ride?" Vanessa questioned.

"I have already told you that they will not let me ride them," Melinda repeated.

"I tell you what we will do," Vanessa said. "You ride Samson and, if I tell him to look after you, he will do so. Then I will ride one of your uncle's horses."

Melinda's eyes lit up immediately.

"Do you really think we can?" she asked.

"We can try. He may say 'no', but, although we don't want to go far today, shall I tell one of the grooms to provide me with a mount, while you ride Samson?"

"He is surely the biggest horse I have ever ridden," Melinda answered. "But I am certain I can control him."

Then Vanessa lifted Melinda onto Samson's back, patted him and said,

"Now be a good boy and show how well you can behave. You are not to race too fast against the horse I will be riding."

"And will he do exactly as you tell him?" Melinda asked.

"I hope he will," Vanessa replied. "He always does what I tell him when I am on his back, but you will have to hold him in so that he does not go too fast. And do tell me if you are afraid or nervous in any way."

"I will not be," Melinda said confidently. "I have ridden all my life and Papa always thought that I was a very good rider."

Vanessa wanted to ask someone why they had not encouraged the girl to ride when she came to live with her uncle especially as he had such fine horses.

Then she told herself that they had obviously been extremely stupid with Melinda.

They had no idea how to inspire or help a girl who was finding it difficult to settle down in a strange place.

There was still no sign of anyone in charge in the stables when eventually, mounted on an exceptional horse, Vanessa led the way out of the stable gate with Melinda on Samson.

She noted with relief that she was holding her reins correctly and seemed very much at ease in the saddle.

But Samson was a very much bigger horse than she would have ridden before. So she moved slowly into the paddock at the far end of the stables.

"Are you all right?" Vanessa asked Melinda.

"This is such a big horse," she replied. "But I am talking to him as you told me to do and now he seems to understand what I am saying."

"But of course he does," Vanessa said. "I have just told my horse, who I gather is called 'Thunderbolt', that I admire him very much and I hope he will show me what a gentleman he is, as he has on his back a lady he has not met before and he has only just been introduced to her."

Melinda laughed.

"I don't expect that anyone has told Thunderbolt that before, but I have seen Uncle Edward riding him and he is very fast."

"I don't think we ought to race the two horses too much today," Vanessa said, "as Samson has come quite a long way to meet you. So I think that we should take them for a gentle trot round the paddock."

She smiled as she added,

"Then, if you know the way into the field beyond it, we can let them go a little faster. You must remember that this is the first time I have ridden Thunderbolt, so I have to get used to him."

She only hoped as she spoke that Melinda was as good a rider as she appeared to be.

'If I injure the girl the moment I arrive', Vanessa thought, 'the Marquis will certainly not keep me here very long.'

The horses, however, seemed to know that they had to behave perfectly.

They rounded the paddock and then rode through the gate at the end into a large empty field that any rider would rejoice at finding.

It was then that Vanessa gave Thunderbolt his head.

And Samson was clearly determined that he would not be beaten.

They rode, despite Vanessa's efforts to be sensible, quicker and quicker until they reached the end of a very long field.

The horses were both panting, but Vanessa was still sitting sideways on Thunderbolt and Melinda was safely on Samson.

"That was marvellous," Melinda said. "I have never ridden such a big horse or so fast, but he did exactly as I told him and I was riding as fast as you."

"You were indeed. Now I think, as Samson has had a long day already, that we should go quietly home and, of course, if you will show me a different way to go, it will be interesting for me to see more of the grounds that we will explore every day, otherwise Samson might complain."

Melinda giggled.

"We must not upset Samson, must we?"

"Of course not!" Vanessa replied. "As you are such an excellent rider, you will have a large choice of horses to inspect and then decide which one you like the best."

"I am sure I would not have been allowed to do so if you had not given the orders," Melinda answered. "I was thinking just now, when you told the groom to saddle Thunderbolt, that he might refuse."

Vanessa did not tell her that she was used to giving orders and that she gave them in a way that few servants would refuse to obey.

'Maybe,' she thought to herself, 'I am overstepping my position as Governess, but it has been everything to get the girl on my side and his Lordship should be grateful for that.'

Although she would not say so, she felt that they had been very stupid in allowing Melinda to become so worked up about her Governesses.

The ones that his Lordship had chosen for her had obviously always been the hard-faced and possessive type of Governesses who thought that the world was made for them to walk on and, because they were teaching children, they believed that everyone had an inferior brain to theirs.

'All I wanted when I was young,' Vanessa thought, 'was my mother's love and the excitement of living, which so many people forget children need as much as grown-ups.'

She therefore talked excitedly to Melinda of what they would do in the future.

"You must ride your uncle's horses until you find one you really love and who loves you," she said. "Then we will try all sorts of things including racing and jumping and teaching the horses to be at their best when we try to show people how splendid they are."

"It will be such great fun," Melinda replied. "But supposing Uncle Edward does not let me ride his horses? I was indeed afraid that the groom would refuse to saddle Thunderbolt for you."

Vanessa had been afraid too.

But, because Melinda had chosen Thunderbolt for her, he had not protested or suggested another horse.

Despite his name Thunderbolt had indeed behaved beautifully.

When they returned to The Castle, Vanessa was not surprised to see the Marquis standing in the stables talking to the two grooms who had saddled their horses.

"'Ere they come, my Lord," she heard the older man say as they turned in at the gate.

She saw the surprise on his Lordship's face when they rode nearer to him as he first saw Samson, who had always surprised people with his sheer size.

His surprise then turned to astonishment as he saw Melinda on his back and Vanessa on one of his largest and fastest horses.

"We have had a lovely ride, my Lord," Vanessa said, before he could speak. "I have been congratulating your niece on the excellent way she rides. She has had no trouble at all with Samson, who I think has enjoyed it as much as she has."

"That's true," Melinda agreed, who had drawn up beside her uncle. "He is such a beautiful horse and he has listened to every word I have said to him."

The Marquis looked surprised, but was too tactful to say anything.

He merely patted Samson on his neck as his niece jumped down off him.

Vanessa let the groom lead Samson away.

"I have admired your horses very much," she said. "I hope you will allow Melinda to ride with me every day. It's the best exercise one can get and a lesson which I think is essential for everyone and especially for those who have to travel."

She saw the Marquis's eyes twinkle and knew that he had understood what she was inferring.

Then, as she jumped off Thunderbolt, he said,

"If Thunderbolt behaved exactly as you wanted him to, then you are obviously a very experienced rider."

"I would hope I am," Vanessa answered. "I have been riding ever since I can remember and your niece and I want to try all the horses in the stables before we decide which one is the best and the most exciting."

She realised that Melinda was listening attentively to what she was saying and she hoped that the Marquis would have the good sense to understand.

Almost to her surprise he did.

"But, of course!" he exclaimed. "If my stables are to become a schoolroom, then they are at your disposal and, if you teach the horses as well as your pupil, I will, of course, offer prizes at the end of the term!"

Vanessa laughed as he obviously meant her to do.

To his amusement Melinda laughed too.

"I hope it will be a very big prize," she cried, "and I am determined to win it!"

"That is just what I was going to say about myself," Vanessa replied, "and, if it is a dead heat at the end, we will just have to share the prize between us."

Melinda looked at her uncle.

"What is the prize to be?" she quizzed him.

"That is a secret," he answered. "And a lot depends on if I am allowed to compete too or if you are keeping the game to yourselves."

"So I would suggest," Vanessa said before Melinda could speak, "that your Lordship should then have to be handicapped in some way, but we will work that out. You must give us time to practice and that we will do every day until we are prepared to take part in the Grand National if necessary!"

The Marquis laughed.

"There is nothing like being ambitious and I accept your challenge, Miss Dawson."

"Now we will have to work hard," Vanessa said to Melinda.

"I will be determined to beat him," she answered, "and, as you said, we will try every horse until we find out which is the fastest of them all."

She said the last words quietly.

Vanessa smiled.

"Keep it a secret for the moment," she whispered, "otherwise they might send me away."

Melinda's eyes widened.

"They must not do that," she said. "I want you to stay here and to ride with me."

"That is just what I want to do," Vanessa replied, "but it would be a mistake to say so too soon."

The girl understood and nodded her head.

Vanessa then patted Thunderbolt again and let him be taken away into the stables.

The Marquis was looking surprised as if he could hardly comprehend what had happened.

Then Vanessa said,

"Now, as I am sure that it's time for tea, we must go back to the house. By the way, I hope your Lordship will allow me to explore your magnificent Castle."

"I am sure that Melinda will be delighted to show you round," he replied. "But there are a few things I would like to talk to you about, Miss Dawson."

Then, reaching out her hand to Melinda, who had just joined them, Vanessa said,

"Come along! I expect Samson and Thunderbolt will be having their tea now and that is what we need too. I am certain that you are as hungry as I am."

As she was talking, she had taken the girl's hand and they were moving away before the Marquis could say anything more.

Only when they were out of sight of the stables did Vanessa exclaim,

"We have won! We have won! He never said a word against you riding his horses and now we can really race each other."

"Are you quite sure that Uncle Edward will let us?" Melinda asked. "I was terrified when I saw him in the yard that he would forbid me to ride one of his big horses."

"I will ensure that he does not stop you," Vanessa answered. "But we must make him think that we are doing our lessons exactly as he would expect us to do, otherwise he may send me away."

The girl's hand tightened on hers.

"I want you to stay," she cried. "You must not go away. You are very different from the other Governesses who have come here."

"You cannot be certain they did not have something hidden that you could well have enjoyed," Vanessa replied. "Quite frankly you are helping me and I am very grateful."

"You mean that you are still frightened that people might find you and take you away?" Melinda enquired.

"They might and so we must be on the lookout for them and I can hide when I see them coming."

"I will hide you," Melinda said, "and there are lots of wonderful hiding places in The Castle where they would never think of looking for you."

"That is just what I want you to show me, Melinda, and don't forget that we will have to think of lessons that will impress your uncle."

"What have I learnt today?" Melinda asked.

"You ought to tell me that, but, as it's your very first lesson, I would say that you have learnt that horses understand what you are saying to them and that the faster you go the quicker you can think."

Melinda laughed and they were still laughing when they went upstairs towards the schoolroom.

CHAPTER SIX

They had finished what Vanessa thought was a very 'nursery' tea.

There were thick sandwiches and a cake, which she was certain the servants downstairs would not have thought good enough for themselves.

Melinda drank her tea and then piped up,

"What shall we do now?"

"What I would like," Vanessa answered, "is for you to show me The Castle. If we look at the paintings, we can then decide which ones will be suitable for our next history lesson."

"Paintings!" Melinda exclaimed.

"But of course. There is a marvellous story behind all the important paintings and, if I cannot think of a good one, you will have to invent one for me!"

They both laughed at this and they then set off on a tour of The Castle.

To Vanessa it was even more fascinating than she had thought it would be.

She was very impressed first by the State bedrooms that all boasted carved and decorated four-poster beds and one even had a gold carved canopy with angels climbing up it.

"This is a lovely, lovely Castle!" Vanessa cried out. "It's such a pity it's not filled with lots and lots of people."

"When Mama was alive, I believe they had parties every week," Melinda told her. "But Uncle Edward is only interested in riding and hardly ever gives a party here."

Vanessa thought that this was strange, but she did not say so.

Eventually, after looking at the drawing room, the writing room and several beautiful reception rooms that were large enough to hold a crowd of people, they reached the music room.

Vanessa took one look at the grand piano, which was standing on a platform and clapped her hands.

"I thought you would have one in The Castle!" she exclaimed. "Next to the library I would say that this is a very significant room for you."

"For me?" Melinda questioned.

"Yes, of course," Vanessa replied. "You must have parties here and dance."

"I have never danced since I came here," Melinda said miserably.

"Well, dance now. I really want to see how good you are."

She sat down at the piano and Melinda started to twirl round to the music.

She threw out her arms and danced quite well on her toes.

"You did that beautifully," Vanessa said, softening the music a little. "If only you had a partner, which you ought to have, and then I could play all sorts of new dances for you."

Even as she spoke the door opened and the Marquis came in.

"I wondered who was playing the piano," he began.

"You are just the person we want," Vanessa told him. "Will your Lordship please ask the lovely lady on the floor without a partner if she will dance a waltz with you?"

She thought for just a moment that the Marquis was going to refuse. Then, as if he thought it extraordinary, he turned towards his niece and smiled,

"I had no idea you danced, Melinda."

"Of course she dances very well," Vanessa said. "I am playing one of the very latest waltzes for you that I hear is a great success in London."

As she spoke, she played the waltz very loudly so that it would be difficult if the Marquis wanted to argue for her to hear him.

Rather reluctantly he put out his arms and Melinda started to waltz with him.

He danced beautifully.

He had obviously danced, as most men of his age had, from the time he had left Oxford and was pursued by all the women who wanted to marry him for his title.

Vanessa quickened the pace of the music a little and they went faster and faster round the room.

Eventually she brought them to a standstill and the Marquis said,

"I had no idea that you were a dancer. But now I do remember that your mother was a particularly good at tripping 'the light fantastic'."

"She taught me to dance soon after I could walk," Melinda answered him. "She used to have parties which I could hear in the nursery and I was sometimes allowed to peep through from the balcony in the ballroom at her."

"I am sure that your uncle will want to give a party for you," Vanessa suggested. "There must be a lot of boys and girls of your age living round here."

"A party!" the Marquis quizzed.

"Of course," Vanessa replied. "I think it would be wise for her to continue her dancing, which she is so good at and there must be plenty of people you could ask, my Lord."

The Marquis stared at her.

For a moment she thought that he was going to defy her and say that he had no wish to have children dancing in his ballroom.

Then, before he could speak, she said,

"Of course it is all part of her education. Every girl must dance well before she 'comes out'. I expect you will remember that if they are bad dancers they quickly become wallflowers."

As she spoke, she knew from the expression on his face that she had won another victory, although he longed to refute the idea.

"You have agreed! You have agreed!" Melinda said excitedly. "It will be fun if Miss Dawson could also find us a band."

The Marquis drew in his breath.

Vanessa, because she was afraid that he was going to say that he would not have a band in The Castle, said quickly,

"As there are one or two things I wish to ask you about, my Lord, could we go out onto the terrace while Melinda practices her steps or shows me if she can play anything on the piano?"

"I can play," Melinda answered. "Not very well, but I can play a little piece that Mama taught me."

She climbed up onto the platform as she spoke and Vanessa passed her the piano stool.

As soon as Melinda sat down at the piano, Vanessa walked towards the window and the Marquis followed her.

There they could not be overheard by the girl, who was slowly picking out a simple tune that Vanessa guessed she had learnt two or three years ago.

"I had no idea that she was interested in anything musical," the Marquis said before Vanessa could speak.

She was sure that he was feeling rather ashamed of himself that this had been unknown to him.

"I have a great deal more to discover about her," Vanessa replied, "than I have done already. But one thing which I think is very important is that she is twelve years of age, but is being treated as if she was still in the nursery and eating nursery food at every meal."

The Marquis stared at her.

"What do you suggest?" he asked.

"When you are alone, as you are at the moment," Vanessa replied, "I think that she should have luncheon with you. After all children in other families always have luncheon with their parents if they are at home. So it is not surprising that Melinda was difficult when she had no one but a Governess to talk to."

The Marquis smiled unexpectedly.

"That rather depends on the Governess. And I can see that she enjoys being with you."

"Not at mealtimes," Vanessa said.

"Very well, I invite you both to luncheon tomorrow and I will give orders that in future Melinda has her meals downstairs in the dining room."

He paused for a moment before he went on,

"I would presume if I have grown-ups that she will not expect to have dinner with them?"

"There is no reason why she should have dinner with you, if you don't want her to," Vanessa replied. "But luncheon is different. I know it is correct for her to have

110

luncheon in the dining room and that is where she would be if her father and mother were alive."

"I think I am right in saying," the Marquis retorted, "that Governesses also have luncheon in the dining room."

"It does not matter to me one way or the other," Vanessa answered. "But I am thinking of Melinda."

"I know you are and I am very grateful for it," the Marquis replied. "I tell you what we will do. Tomorrow when we start this new regime, as I will be alone, I will ask you to luncheon *and* dinner. At least that will be a variety for my niece and we will see if she appreciates it."

He walked back to the music room as he spoke.

Vanessa was sure that he was thinking how difficult Melinda had been and how the Governesses had rushed away from The Castle refusing to stay longer with a child they thought utterly impossible to teach.

"She must have music lessons," Vanessa remarked, "because she obviously likes music and I hope in the next day or two to find out what other subjects really interest her."

"I think that you have done marvels already," the Marquis sighed. "In the past by this time a Governess I had engaged was scowling and it was only a question of time before she gave in her notice and left."

"I hope to be the exception to that rule," Vanessa replied. "Now please make a list of any children of her age who we can invite to a party. I think a small band they can dance to and have a cotillion would be something to look forward to."

The Marquis threw up his hands.

"You are going too fast!" he complained. "You are leaving me breathless, Miss Dawson, but, of course, I will consider anything you suggest."

"That at any rate is a step in the right direction," Vanessa said. "I am only sorry that she has upset you and been exceedingly unhappy when in such a beautiful Castle there should only be happiness and laughter."

Again the Marquis looked at her in surprise.

But she had turned and was gazing at Melinda who had just finished playing the little tune she had learnt.

"That was particularly nice," Vanessa said walking towards her. "As you played so well, your uncle has asked us both to have luncheon with him tomorrow in the dining room."

"Oh, that will be fun if you are there!" Melinda exclaimed. "I am sure that Uncle Edward does not eat the dull meals which are brought up to us."

"I would be surprised if he did," Vanessa answered with her eyes twinkling.

She turned towards the Marquis and realised that he was looking slightly ashamed of himself.

As if he wanted to change the subject, he then said to Melinda,

"I saw you riding on Miss Dawson's horse today. I should have thought that he would have been too much for you and you would have been content with a pony."

"I have not ridden a pony since I was six," Melinda answered indignantly. "Papa let me ride all his horses and, although they were not as good as Thunderbolt, I could go very fast on them."

"The trouble has been," the Marquis said as if he must excuse himself, "I was not told anything about you until you arrived. I see now that we should have sat down and made a list of what you could do and what you wanted to do."

"Now I just want to do things with Miss Dawson," Melinda said, "and she taught me this morning to talk to

Samson and I think he understood everything I was saying to him."

"That is certainly a step forward," the Marquis said looking at Vanessa.

"It is something I learnt as soon as I began to ride," she replied. "My father believes that the reason his horses have been so successful is because he tells them what he expects them to do before a race begins."

The Marquis stared at her in astonishment.

"Your father has racing horses!" he queried.

Vanessa realised that she had made a mistake and so she said quickly,

"I think it is something we should discuss another time. Now Melinda is going to dance for you to a very different tune and I am sure, if you will watch her, you will see that she has the chance of being an outstanding dancer before she is very much older."

Not only the Marquis but Melinda were listening to her with surprise.

Then Melinda asked as Vanessa came towards the piano,

"How shall I dance?"

"Dance as you were dancing just now when I was playing," Vanessa told her. "I thought how pretty it looked in the sun coming in through the windows and you looked like a fairy hovering over the flowers."

She saw that Melinda was now about to refuse to dance for her uncle.

But because she could not resist the music which Vanessa began to play, she went very reluctantly into the centre of the room.

The Marquis had seated himself on an armchair and Vanessa was sure that he was thinking that this was the most unusual and extraordinary scenario that he had ever known.

As it was important that he should be impressed with his niece, Vanessa struck the piano with gusto.

Then she burst into a gay and fast tune that had been a great success, her father had told her, in London when it was played to an audience at *The Gaiety*.

It was heard by all the beautiful women who were pursued by the smartest and best-dressed men in the Social world.

If the Marquis was surprised to hear it in his music room, Melinda found it inspiring, as Vanessa knew that she would.

She started to dance wildly in time to the music.

Although it was clearly a childish and exaggerated exhibition, it was, Vanessa knew well, something that the Marquis had not expected.

To Melinda it was more exciting than anything she had ever known, but she was, however, clever enough to realise what the music expected of her.

And when Vanessa finished playing, Melinda sank to the ground in a deep and elaborate curtsey.

As if he just could not help himself, the Marquis clapped his hands.

"Now we must certainly have a party, as you have suggested," he proposed. "Or perhaps it should be a stage performance!"

There was just a touch of irony in his last words.

Vanessa, rising from the piano stool, laughed.

"I think it would surprise the neighbourhood too much," she said. "Although I do think that Melinda will be a marvellous dancer one day, we had better keep the party respectable and I am sure that there is a local band that would play exactly the right tunes so that no one would be shocked."

"They would certainly be surprised at hearing what you have just played to us here in my house," the Marquis answered.

"Then I think it is something I should play again and again so that the gloom is swept away and the whole building vibrates to the fun and frolic of those who admire it," Vanessa retorted.

"Fun and frolic has never occurred here," he said.

"I wonder if that is true," Vanessa answered. "You go back a great number of years and I cannot believe that Queen Elizabeth, when she was staying here, did not ask for music that made her want to dance. And, if Charles II was another visitor, it would most certainly not have been a gloomy evening for him."

"I can easily see that your history lessons will be unusual," the Marquis commented somewhat sarcastically.

"Miss Dawson told me two stories today," Melinda said, "about the paintings and I found both of them very very interesting."

"And it was, of course, our history lesson," Vanessa answered somewhat primly, "and I think you will find that your niece enjoys a good story in the same way everyone else does."

She spoke in a tone that told the Marquis without words that he should have found out about it before.

Then he said,

"I see, Miss Dawson, that your ideas and the way you teach are different from the usual where a Governess is concerned and I will be most interested to see the final result."

"I can only hope that your Lordship will not be disappointed," Vanessa answered.

The Marquis walked towards the door.

"I will certainly think over what you have told me," he replied, "and I am looking forward to seeing you both at luncheon tomorrow at one o'clock."

He was gone before Vanessa could think of a reply.

Then she held out her hands and swung Melinda round and round on the polished floor.

"We have won! We have won!" she cried. "I am determined that you shall have a party here and, when we come down to dinner tomorrow night, he is going to find you a very interesting and exciting girl."

"How will he do that?" Melinda asked her a little breathlessly.

"We will have to think out a way of surprising him. I think he has been very unimaginative in providing you with endless boring Governesses so that you have had to drive them away almost before they even arrived."

Melinda giggled.

"They were ugly, dull and determined to make me as unpleasant as they were themselves," she said.

"So do you find that I am different?" Vanessa asked as they came to a standstill.

"Of course you are different. I just knew when you were riding a horse that you were different from those silly old women, who are much too frightened to ride anything. And they talked to me as if I was as dull and dreary as they were."

"Well, I am very determined that you shall have a wonderful time and be a huge success when you grow up so that your uncle will be proud of you."

"I expect, although he has talked to you, that he is far too busy with the women who run after him to think about me," Melinda said.

Vanessa stared at her.

"What do you mean by that?"

"Oh, I have heard the servants talking! They were always telling my old Nanny before she left and then the Governesses how Uncle Edward is totally determined not to marry simply because he realises that women make such a fuss of him because he is a Marquis."

Vanessa did not say anything for a moment.

Then she said,

"Now I understand why he likes to be alone. But I am sorry for him and we must do our best to cheer him up and make him feel happy."

"That will be fun," Melinda answered, "if you can think of new things for him to do."

"Of course I can. I promise you, your uncle will cheer up and then want to fill this house with amusing and attractive people instead of sitting here all alone obviously disliking everyone in the world outside."

"But he is grown up," Melinda said, "and, if he wanted to ask people here, he could ask them."

"Perhaps he does not know anyone except those who have run after him for his title," Vanessa answered. "We need to show him, you and me, that we are not the least bit interested in his title and we want to laugh and have fun and, of course, ride those beautiful fast horses."

There was a moment's pause.

Then Melinda flung her arms around Vanessa and squeezed her, saying,

"Thank you! Thank you so much for coming here! Now everything is so different. I was so unhappy until you came."

She hesitated before she went on,

"I used to talk to Mama when I was in bed and tell her that she must come back and make things happy for Uncle Edward. But now I believe that she must have sent *you*."

Vanessa bent down and kissed Melinda's cheek.

"You are quite right," she said. "I feel sure that your mother would want him to be happy and you to be happy too.

"I am happy since you came, Miss Dawson. You are so nice and such fun. Do let's think of more and more lovely things to do."

"We have done a great deal already today and now we have to plan for tomorrow. We have to think about interesting subjects we can discuss with your uncle while we are having luncheon in the dining room. I am sure that he is expecting us to sit there quietly because we are so over-awed by him."

Melinda laughed.

"We must think of things we can talk about that will surprise him," she suggested.

"We will do that, but we must put on our thinking caps and decide what they should be."

Vanessa smiled at Melinda as she went on,

"Now have one more dance before we go upstairs. While you are having your bath, we will start to think out all the things we know a great deal about which your uncle has not thought about before."

"Yes, that is what we will do!" Melinda exclaimed in delight. "It will be exciting because I am doing it with you."

When they went upstairs to the schoolroom, there was again a dull nursery supper as there had been the night before.

Vanessa was quite certain that it was prepared by one of the kitchenmaids rather than the cook and a footman brought the tray upstairs, but he did not wait on them.

It was while they were eating the dull food that Vanessa said after a short silence,

"I have thought of something. We have persuaded your uncle to ask us to dinner. Then we will dress up like some of his ancestors. I am sure that somewhere in this large Castle there is a collection of dresses that have been handed down through the centuries."

"I know the housekeeper has some," Melinda said, "because I heard her say once that when Uncle Edward's mother was alive she had very beautiful dresses."

She paused before she went on excitedly,

"She had a lot of them upstairs in the attics with the clothes she keeps for the Nativity play they always had here at Christmas."

"Good!" Vanessa exclaimed, "That is exactly what I wanted! Now you be charming to your uncle tomorrow at luncheon and I will think out a conversation that at the very least will make him laugh."

"You are very clever," Melinda said, "and I am so looking forward to it all. But will we still ride in the morning?"

"Of course we will. I am determined that Samson will be faster than any horse your uncle owns."

"That might make him cross," Melinda said rather apprehensively.

"On the contrary," Vanessa replied. "I think he will go to Tattersalls to buy some more horses which we will enjoy too when they come."

They were both laughing when they walked into Melinda's bedroom. It was a child's room, rather dull and over-clean.

Vanessa made a secret vow to see that she was moved into a larger and more impressive room.

'If he treats her as a naughty child,' she thought, 'it is undoubtedly what she will become. At twelve, as far as I can remember, I was beginning to have grown up ideas and that is what I must fight for Melinda to have.'

*

The next day, in case they were stopped, Vanessa made Melinda hurry through her breakfast and reach the stables before her uncle appeared.

She felt that it would be prudent, as Thunderbolt was undoubtedly his favourite horse, that Melinda should ride something different.

There was another horse that she had noticed at once and she was not surprised to hear the Head Groom say that it was another of his Lordship's special favourites.

He was rather doubtful when Vanessa ordered him to saddle it, but, as she pointed out, she was quite certain that his Lordship would want to ride Thunderbolt.

"Now I thinks 'bout it, 'is Lordship did mention it yesterday," the Head Groom admitted.

Vanessa looked at Melinda and said,

"Yesterday you rode my horse, now I am going to ride my own and you can choose any one you want except, of course, Thunderbolt. I think that you should leave him for your uncle."

Melinda gave a little jump for joy.

"Then I want Sunshine," she cried. "I have always thought he is one of the prettiest horses Uncle possesses, but the groom would not let me ride him."

"If you can ride my horse, then you are capable of riding any horse in the stables," Vanessa pointed out.

She was looking at the Head Groom as she spoke and, as he did not want to be brought into the argument, he saddled Sunshine and lifted Melinda onto him.

Another groom had by now saddled Samson and, as they then rode out from the yard side by side, the Marquis appeared at the other entrance.

Seeing his niece on Sunshine, he walked up to the Head Groom and said angrily,

"That horse is far too large and fast for the child. You have no right to let her mount him."

"It be the Governess's orders, your Lordship," the groom replied. "I thinks your Lordship'd be surprised 'ow well the young lady can ride. She were as fast as that other 'orse which be one of the finest I've ever seen."

The Marquis with difficulty did not reply.

He rode into the paddock and to his astonishment his niece and her Governess were putting their horses at the jumps that he had had raised a few weeks ago for himself.

As they took the first jump, he drew in his reins and sat waiting for them to fall or some other danger to occur.

Then to his great surprise they both took the jumps without any difficulty.

They were, he realised, racing each other round the course and, because he knew that it would be a mistake and dangerous to stop them, he stopped under some trees.

They passed him without being aware that he was there.

They were striving to beat each other and, as both their horses were outstanding, it was not an easy task.

In fact when he followed them on the outside of the course expecting at any moment for there to be a disaster, they reached the Winning Post.

Melinda won by a head, although he was somewhat suspicious that Miss Dawson had let her do so.

"I have won! I have won!" Melinda was shouting with joy as he joined them.

"You rode splendidly," Vanessa said. "I am sure that your uncle will be very proud of you."

She had been aware that the Marquis was following them and, as she suspected, he was looking concerned.

Then, as if he could hardly believe what he had seen was real, he said,

"I must congratulate you both. I had no idea that Melinda could ride so well."

"I always rode Papa's horses," Melinda pointed out. "But when I came here, I was told I had to ride a pony."

She spoke hastily and the Marquis said,

"You should have come and told me yourself that you had ridden your father's horses which were all superb. I can only apologise for the fact that the household did not expect you to ride as I have just seen you."

He smiled before he added,

"Now I can only give you my congratulations and say that your father would have been very proud of you."

Vanessa thought he had, at least, behaved decently and done what was expected of him.

"I think that Papa would have been proud to ride this horse himself," Melinda said after a moment.

"Of course he would," the Marquis agreed. "He always helped me choose the horses when I was buying them and every horse he selected as a winner always won!"

"Well, he would be so proud of you now, Melinda," Vanessa said, "and Samson is furious that you beat him at the last moment. He is used to always winning every race he enters, but now he must admit that Sunshine was a nose and a half ahead of him."

Melinda laughed at that.

"It's lucky he has a very big nose," she replied. "If it was my nose, no one would have noticed it."

"That is true enough," Vanessa chipped in. "But perhaps we can buy you a false one that you can use when you are riding in a race and then you could say that you were a nose ahead and no one would be able to argue!"

Melinda laughed again and, as if he could not help himself, the Marquis laughed too.

"What I suggest we do," he said, "as we are all on spectacular horses, is to have a race. I propose that we now go into the orchard as the field beyond it is one of the best places I have always found for racing."

"The three of us!" Melinda cried excitedly. "That is something new and I am very sure that Sunshine will be determined to win."

"Then he will have to pull up his socks," her uncle replied, "for the good reason that Thunderbolt always wins his races and would be humiliated and doubtless in tears if he is beaten."

"We will have to risk that," Melinda giggled.

"I am really sure that your uncle will have a prize for everyone," Vanessa remarked, "and none of our horses must be hurt or upset because they are not the first past the Post."

"I just knew that you would have an answer to that difficulty," the Marquis replied.

"I only hope that you have the prizes, my Lord," Vanessa responded.

They rode out to the field beyond the orchard.

The ground was firm and it was at least a mile long.

As they rode to what he called the 'Starting Post', the Marquis said to Vanessa in a whisper,

"Do you think we ought to give Melinda a start?"

"I think it would be insulting for that particular horse. She is thrilled to be treated as if she was grown up and, as she has been pushed more or less into the nursery since she arrived here, I want you to accept her as an equal, anyway on occasions such as this."

"Of course you are right," the Marquis agreed. "I have the unfortunate feeling that you are *always* right."

"I hope I am where Melinda is concerned," Vanessa answered. "And I have discovered why she has been so difficult and unhappy since she came to live with you."

"I know I am going to be rebuked for that," the Marquis murmured, "if for nothing else!"

"It's quite easy to make up for it," Vanessa retorted.

"All I can do is to promise you that I will try," he said. "Is that enough?"

"Very nearly, my Lord, but I daresay I will be like the persistent beggar and always ask for more!"

The Marquis laughed.

As they then joined Melinda at the Starting Post, all three were smiling.

The Marquis gave the signal to go and they started off, each of them wildly anxious to be declared the winner.

It was a race, Vanessa reflected afterwards, which was almost perfect.

The sun was shining and she felt that the other two were as happy as she was and the horses were striving in every possible way to win.

It was with difficulty that she and the Marquis held their horses back so that just by a short nose Melinda was the winner.

"I have won! I have won!" she screamed out with excitement.

The Marquis and Vanessa both agreed that she had ridden brilliantly.

In fact, as they rode back to The Castle, she had never known three people to be quite as happy as they were except, of course, the horses were happier still!

Luncheon was a great success, Vanessa thought.

Not only were they talking about their horses but the Marquis became much more human when he told them about the most unusual places abroad where he had raced on all sorts of strange animals.

When he returned, he had been glad to be back on his own horses that Vanessa realised that he prized them more than anything else.

All the same it seemed to her odd that he should want to be alone in his huge Castle with its magnificent stables rather than entertaining people of his own age.

Of course women would pursue him not only for his title but because he was very good-looking,

Also, when he wished to be, he was very witty and entertaining.

Luncheon was a meal that both she and Melinda enjoyed, not only because there were plenty of delicious dishes to eat but because the conversation was scintillating.

It was only when it finished that the Marquis said,

"I have to go out this afternoon unfortunately, but I think, as our conversation was such fun, that we should continue it at dinner tonight."

"Dinner!" Melinda exclaimed. "Oh, I would love to come down to dinner with you, Uncle Edward."

"Then I will expect you both at eight o'clock and, if you are tired tomorrow, Melinda, because you are late to bed, you must not blame me."

"I will not be tired and I would love to have dinner with you," Melinda said excitedly. "I am sick of being put to bed having had nothing to eat but rice pudding or cheese sandwiches."

"You will most certainly have better tonight," the Marquis promised.

When he left the room, Vanessa suggested,

"Now is our chance to surprise your uncle. Let's go and find Mrs. Shepherd and see what she has upstairs for us."

"You mean we can have dinner with him in fancy dress?" Melinda asked.

"Of course we can. We have to surprise him and make him enjoy life instead of sitting at the table gloomily all by himself."

She had already heard from a talkative housemaid how dull they found The Castle after the Marquis had been upset when his fiancée had run away with another man.

"Because people talked and, of course, laughed at 'im behind their 'ands," the housemaid had said, 'e never goes to London, but stays 'ere all the time buryin' 'imself in the country."

"What we have to do," Vanessa said to Melinda, "is to make your uncle laugh and enjoy himself."

She paused before she went on,

"I suggest you dress up as Queen Elizabeth who I told you about in the painting yesterday and who stayed here once when she was travelling around England."

It was typical, she thought, that no one had told the girl that the Queen had actually stayed at The Castle or that her name was on the door of one of the bedrooms.

It was furnished, Mrs. Shepherd had told her, just as it had been when the Queen had come to visit them.

126

When she was told that they wanted fancy dress, the old housekeeper was delighted.

"Now come upstairs and have a look at what I've got in the attic," she proposed.

When they saw the huge amount of items that had been accumulated over the centuries, Vanessa was thrilled and so was Melinda.

There were dresses of every sort and a profusion of armour for the men in one corner.

One room in the attic was devoted to costumes for Nativity plays that were acted over Christmas and had been the tradition for over three hundred years at The Castle

"I would like Miss Melinda to be dressed as Queen Elizabeth," Vanessa said.

It was not difficult to find the lovely dress in which Melinda looked outstandingly pretty, at the same time very grown up.

There was jewellery for her to wear, some real and some false, and there was also a coronet that might easily have been a crown.

"So what are you going to wear, Miss Dawson?" Melinda then asked when she was finally dressed and was delighted with the reflection of herself in the big mirror.

"I am going to be your Lady-in-Waiting," Vanessa told her. "So what I want is a pretty dress, but nothing so grand and as Royal as yours."

When they had chosen their dresses, taken them to their bedrooms and changed for dinner to the delight of the housekeeper, Vanessa was sure that the Marquis would be extremely surprised.

In fact the whole household was most amused and delighted by what was happening.

The Marquis was waiting in his study with a bottle of champagne in the ice-cooler, when the butler formally announced,

"Her Majesty the Queen Elizabeth of England, my Lord!"

He turned round in astonishment.

When Melinda swept into the room, glittering with jewels and with a dress that had a train, for a moment he thought that he must be dreaming.

She seemed as if she was, in fact, someone Royal.

Then, when he realised that it was indeed his niece, he played his part by bowing and welcoming her by kissing her hand.

Vanessa then heard the butler announce,

"Lady Vanessa Dawson, my Lord."

She swept in, looking very lovely, although she had not actually bothered very much about herself as she had concentrated on Melinda.

Her dress was right for the part and she wore a small wreath of flowers on her fair hair and a long diamond necklace round her neck.

She had no idea that with the evening sun glittering on her wreath and her golden hair and dressed in a low-cut evening gown of a soft blue that matched her eyes, she was the picture that any artist would have wanted to project on canvas.

As the Marquis bowed over her hand in the same way he had over Melinda's, she curtseyed low and said,

"This is a great privilege, my Lord."

"And it is a party I will greatly enjoy," the Marquis answered.

The evening was a great success and it seemed as if every word they said made them all laugh.

It was with difficulty that the butler and footmen kept their dignity and did not laugh with them too.

To Vanessa's surprise the Marquis took them to the music room after dinner.

Whilst he and Melinda waltzed around the room, despite her long train, which had to be hitched up for her, Vanessa played the piano.

It was only when finally Melinda said that she was tired and wanted to go to bed that, as they walked towards the door, the Marquis said in a voice that only Vanessa could hear,

"Come back when my niece is in bed. I want to talk to you."

For a moment she looked at him in surprise.

Then she realised that, as a Governess, it was an order.

And, although it might give the servants something to talk about, she knew that she must obey him.

CHAPTER SEVEN

After she had put Melinda to bed, Vanessa went downstairs again as she had been told.

She found the Marquis in one of the comfortable sitting rooms.

She would have gone to the music room, but the door was open and she saw him waiting for her.

She went in and he motioned for her to sit down on the sofa while he sat in one of the armchairs.

"I think the time has come," he began, "for you to tell me about yourself. I know so little about you and quite frankly I want to know more."

Vanessa smiled.

"There is really very little to tell you," she replied. "Except that I wanted a job and I was told that you had a vacancy, my Lord."

"I want to know much more than that," the Marquis answered.

Vanessa thought that it would be a mistake for her to say too much, so she said,

"I left my home because I did not get on with my stepmother. I was going North to stay with some relations. However, I was told by a very kind man, who was also riding a magnificent horse, that there was a vacancy here, so here I am."

The Marquis laughed.

"You are being very evasive," he told her. "But I will not press you. Instead we will talk about horses."

This was a subject that not only pleased Vanessa but she knew a great deal about it.

Her father had always talked to her as if she was a boy and she had ridden with him every day until he went to India.

It had been a considerable blessing, she had always thought, although she did not say so, that her stepmother did not like riding.

So she talked to the Marquis about the horses that had been outstanding the previous year and, while he was obviously surprised by her knowledge, he did not say so.

Finally they talked about the library that Vanessa pointed out to him was not as up to date as it should be.

"How do you know so much and look so young?" he asked.

She laughed.

"I have been very lucky in learning to ride and read younger than most girls do. With the result that they are the two things which interest me most."

"Just as they interest me," the Marquis answered. "I must, however, thank you for a very enjoyable evening before I send you to bed."

Feeling that she was now dismissed, Vanessa rose to her feet.

Then the Marquis said,

"I cannot understand how anyone could allow you, when you are so young and beautiful, to wander about the world alone. Surely you should have at least a servant to accompany you."

"I will tell you the reason I was alone," Vanessa replied. "But it's a long story."

"I cannot help that," the Marquis told her. "I must know, otherwise I shall lie awake all night wondering what you might have told me but did not."

As she could not help herself, she told him how she had run away from her home and had met a man who had wanted to protect her.

The Marquis made no sound so Vanessa continued her story.

She related how the man had thought that her horse was too valuable for her to travel on alone, so he took her under his wing.

She concluded by saying that it was only when she was in danger that the man had thought to bring her to The Castle and had explained to her how the Marquis would hopefully provide a home for her.

The Marquis listened attentively, but did not try to comment.

It was becoming quite late when the Marquis said,

"Thank you for a most enjoyable evening, but I do think that I now ought to send you to bed."

The hours seemed to have just sped by and Vanessa looked at the gold clock in surprise.

"Can I say," Vanessa asked, "how very glad I am to have come here to you, my Lord, and how much I enjoy being with Melinda."

"Just as she enjoys being with you," the Marquis answered. "Now, before I ask you any more questions, go and get your beauty sleep."

"Good night and God bless you," Vanessa said, just as her mother had always said to her.

She did not realise that the Marquis looked after her quizzically.

And there was an expression in his eyes that had never been there before.

*

The next two days they actually saw very little of the Marquis as he had to attend a County Council Meeting, of which he was the Chairman.

The day after there was a Race Meeting in which he was running one of his horses.

Vanessa hoped that he would take his niece with him and that she would be invited too.

But the invitation did not come.

Instead Melinda and she raced each other again on the field beyond the paddock.

Vanessa, however, felt glad the following day when they learnt that the Marquis would be out to luncheon, but was expecting them to have tea with him in the drawing room later in the afternoon.

He had not been to dinner the two previous nights because he had friends at the Racecourse who insisted on him staying.

Vanessa would have been untruthful if she had not admitted that she was disappointed.

She treasured her conversations with the Marquis, she told herself quietly, because they were intelligent and she very much enjoyed arguing with him, even though she had to admit that he usually won the contest.

"Your uncle will be back for tea," she told Melinda over their luncheon. "I think that you should go and ask the cook to make him something out of the ordinary."

She smiled at the girl before she continued,

"When my father returned home after an exhausting day, my mother always tried to have something special for him to eat because she claimed that when he was talking business he ate very little."

She laughed as she added,

"The food at home was very much better and more appetising than anything he would find elsewhere."

Melinda was only too willing to order something delicious that she would enjoy as well as her uncle.

After the dreary nursery teas, everything that they ate downstairs was tempting.

As Vanessa felt the same, she reckoned that they would soon be saying that they were putting on weight and growing a great deal fatter than they had been before.

They went riding again, but Vanessa kept an eye on the time.

They were back at The Castle before four o'clock. They went upstairs and changed from their riding clothes into pretty thin dresses.

Melinda had her own, but Vanessa borrowed one from the housekeeper, who had taken a considerable fancy to Vanessa.

Some of the very attractive dresses that had been worn by the Marquis's mother were cleaned and pressed and they were even altered a little so that Vanessa could wear them.

"You are so very kind to me, Mrs. Shepherd," she said, "and I do love these pretty gowns."

"You certainly looks very beautiful in them," Mrs. Shepherd told her, "and that's the real truth, not just a compliment."

Vanessa laughed.

"I am so grateful to you," she sighed.

Having arranged her hair so that it shone in the sunlight, she went downstairs with Melinda to find that the Marquis had returned.

"You are back! You are back, Uncle Edward!" Melinda cried out and to his surprise she ran forward and kissed him on the cheek.

"I am looking forward to hearing all your news," he said.

They walked into the drawing room and, because it was so hot, the French windows were open onto the lawn outside.

The tea table was waiting for them and, as the cook had promised, there was a selection of delicious small iced cakes that they had not tasted before.

There was a very large one iced in the Marquis's racing colours and decorated with a horse on top of it.

"Is this all for me?" the Marquis asked.

"Of course it is, Uncle Edward," Melinda replied. "We are so glad that you are no longer too busy for us to have dinner with you. Tea has been very dull the last few days while you have been away."

"Well, I am very glad to be back," he replied, "and thank you for this delicious spread."

He was looking at Vanessa as he spoke.

She knew he was telling her that he was well aware that it was her influence which had made Melinda a very different child from the one when she had arrived.

Vanessa sat down at the table and poured out the tea, while Melinda was talking sixteen to the dozen about the horses. And how fast she and Miss Dawson had raced each other.

Then unexpectedly a man appeared at the window.

As they all three turned their heads to see who it was, Vanessa saw to her considerable surprise that it was the Chief Highwayman.

He walked into the room.

Ignoring the Marquis he said to Vanessa,

"I have come to warn you that your stepmother has found out where you are and is on her way to take you back with her."

Vanessa gave a little cry.

"What is this about," the Marquis demanded, "and may I ask who you are?"

"I have told you about him," Vanessa said before the Chief could speak. "This is the man who was so kind to me and sent me to you."

"Then I can only say I am most grateful to you," the Marquis said to the Chief. "Miss Dawson has been a great joy to my niece and indeed to me, but you say that her stepmother is now approaching."

"Oh, you must hide me!" Vanessa cried. "Please, please hide me! I cannot – go back. She hates me – and I hate her. Oh, how did she find out where I was?"

She was speaking in a terrified voice.

Then the Chief spoke up again,

"It was Alfred who told them. Apparently it was your stepmother who he was attempting to rob and Alfred, resentful of being in prison and hoping to maybe get his sentence shortened, then decided to curry favour with your stepmother by telling her that the horse she was following, because it was even more impressive than its rider, was now at the Marquis of Westfield's Castle.

"Therefore, he begged to see Lady Shotworth, who, determined to find you at any cost, visited the prison and heard Alfred's story."

"She must *not* find me here," Vanessa cried.

Turning to the Marquis, she begged,

"Please hide me! Please tell her that you have never heard of me. I cannot go back with her."

Melinda, who had also risen from the tea table, then said to her uncle,

"Do help her, Uncle Edward! Her stepmother is a horrid woman and if she takes Miss Dawson away we will be very sad without her."

"I am most grateful for your warning," the Marquis told the Chief. "I will not allow this lady, whoever she may be, to take Miss Dawson away from us. I will tell the butler to say that we are not at home."

He crossed the room the ring the bell.

At that moment the butler opened the door.

"There's a lady arrived here, my Lord, who insists on seeing you. As I gather that she wants to speak to you privately, I've shown her into the study."

"That was quite right," the Marquis told him.

Then turning round he said,

"Now if you will sit down and continue your tea, I would like to know a little more about this visitor before I converse with her."

"She's Miss Dawson's horrid stepmother," Melinda explained, "who was very cruel to her. She said that she could have nothing more to eat until she had scrubbed the kitchen floor. Miss Dawson was quite right to run away from her and hide here."

She spoke aggressively and then her uncle said,

"I agree with you, Melinda. Now sit down as I have told you to do."

Then turning to the Chief he said,

"I am afraid I don't know your name. But I hope you will join us, especially as you have been kind enough to warn us of the danger approaching us."

"She is here! *She is here now!*" Melinda cried in a frightened voice. "If she takes Miss Dawson away from us, I shall be very unhappy without her."

The Marquis did not answer her as he was waiting for the Chief to speak.

"My name is Bartholomew Camden," he told him. "But I think it would be a mistake to entertain me."

Vanessa put out her hand to touch his arm.

"I told the Marquis that you have been very kind to me and brought me here – as you thought it was dangerous for me to ride about the countryside on such a fine horse as Samson – without anyone to take care of me."

"Did you also tell him who I am?" the Chief asked.

Before she could reply and it was obvious that she did not know what to say, he turned towards the Marquis.

"I will be honest with you, my Lord, and tell you that I am a highwayman."

He stopped, but, as the Marquis did not speak, he continued,

"Miss Dawson found us by accident one evening and, because I thought that it was dangerous for someone so young and so attractive to be riding out alone on such an outstanding horse, I brought her here with me and my companions as far as your estate."

He paused for a moment and then went on,

"It was only then I learnt that one of my men had been captured by the Police and, as I thought it dangerous for her to be seen with me, I sent her to you."

"For which I am extremely grateful," the Marquis replied. "It is also very brave of you to tell me the truth about yourself. I therefore suggest that you have tea with us while I consider what I will say to the lady who wishes to take Miss Dawson from us."

"Oh, please stay!" Melinda pleaded in a soft voice to the Chief.

Vanessa thought that only the Marquis would have been so friendly or so kind.

As they sat down at the table, she smiled at him, but at the same time her hands were shaking as she was so frightened.

She was sure that however much the Marquis might say he wanted her to stay, her stepmother would insist on her returning merely to punish her for running away.

Yet, because she realised that he expected her to behave sensibly, she poured the Chief out a cup of tea and passed it to him.

"Now before I send for the lady who is waiting to tell me all about your misdemeanours," the Marquis said to Vanessa, "will you tell me just why you ran away?"

"My stepmother was forever finding fault with me and she wanted to punish me – by forcing me to scrub the floor in the kitchen, which naturally upset the servants who have been with us for years. So I ran away."

She drew in her breath before she went on,

"When I came here to you, it was on Mr. Camden's insistence that I should not travel North – all on my own."

She hesitated before she went on,

"He was quite right in thinking that Samson is too spectacular not to be noticed. If I had not done what he suggested, I am very sure – that my stepmother would have caught up with me, as she has now, and insisted on my – returning with her."

"Do you really want to stay with us?" the Marquis asked.

"You know – I do, my Lord," Vanessa replied.

"Of course she does," Melinda chimed in. "She is happy here, she said so, and I really want her to stay with us."

"I want that too," the Marquis said quietly. "So now I will tell your stepmother to go away and to let you know when your father returns from India."

As he spoke, he rang a small silver bell, which was on the tea tray.

The door was opened instantly by the butler, who must have been waiting just outside.

"Show the lady in here," the Marquis told him.

"Very good, my Lord," the butler replied.

He went out closing the door and Vanessa said,

"Please hide me! I am sure it would be better if she thought – that I was not here."

"You have to trust me," the Marquis said. "If Mr. Camden has kept you safe until you came here, I will keep you safe until you are ready to go to your relatives in the North."

"I want her to stay with us," Melinda cried. "Oh, Uncle Edward, please make her stay."

"Leave it to me," the Marquis answered.

The door opened and the butler announced.

"The Countess of Shotworth, my Lord."

Vanessa saw the surprise on the Marquis's face and then she remembered that she had not told her real name to anyone.

The Chief was also surprised.

Then, as the Countess came in, the Marquis rose to his feet and said,

"This is a surprise, Lady Shotworth. I had no idea that you were in the vicinity, but I have met your husband many times on the Racecourse. In fact I rather expected him to be at the races yesterday."

"He is in India," the Countess replied sharply. "I am here for a very different reason. I have heard that my tiresome stepdaughter is staying with you and I intend to take her back with me immediately."

"I am afraid that is totally impossible," the Marquis replied. "But do sit down and let me pour you a cup of tea."

"I have no wish for tea or to spend any time here in your Castle," the Countess said harshly. "My stepdaughter has behaved abominably and I will take her home and send for the horse she was riding in the next day or two."

There was silence for a moment and Vanessa felt Melinda's hand slip into hers.

"As I have already told you," the Marquis answered quietly. "It is impossible for your stepdaughter to leave here at the moment. But I will be in touch with her father as soon as he returns from India and I know that he will understand that under the circumstances she cannot leave here at present."

"That is for *me* to say," the Countess snapped. "As I have already said, she is to come with me at once, leaving her horse here until my groom can collect it."

"As I have already said," the Marquis replied, "that is impossible. Her father, when he returns, will understand my reason for saying this."

"If my stepdaughter refuses to do what I tell her," the Countess expostulated, "I will send for the Police as I am her legal Guardian."

"I think that would be a great mistake," the Marquis retorted coldly.

He cleared his throat before he went on,

"The reason that your stepdaughter cannot join you is, for the moment, a secret! But I will certainly make it very clear when anyone asks the reason why she must stay here with me and my niece."

"I have never heard such nonsense in the whole of my life," the Countess said sharply. "I understand Vanessa is here as Governess to your niece and that is very much your business and not mine!"

She added in a very haughty voice,

141

"As my stepdaughter, she has to obey me and leave at once!"

There was an uncomfortable silence and then the Marquis said coldly,

"I have already told you that is impossible! I know you will understand why she cannot leave when I tell you that, although it is for the moment a secret, Vanessa has promised *to be my wife!*"

He spoke slowly and quietly.

But what he said might have been a bomb for the effect it had on those listening.

The Countess stiffened as the Chief looked at the Marquis in amazement.

For a few moments there was complete silence until Melinda jumped up saying,

"Oh, Uncle Edward. You are going to marry Miss Dawson. How really lovely! Please, please can I be a bridesmaid? I am so excited because now she will be my aunt."

She threw herself against Vanessa, putting her arms round her neck as she spoke, and kissed her.

For a moment no one else moved.

Then the Countess turned round and stalked out of the room, slamming the door behind her.

It was only when she was out of earshot did the Chief laugh.

"That was a winning blow, if ever there was one," he remarked.

The Marquis turned towards him and said,

"I have already heard just how interested you are in horses and that you recognised Samson at once for what he is."

The Chief did not reply and he went on,

"It just happened that before I came in for tea, my Head Groom told me that he had been offered a job at the Racecourse, which is just what he has always wanted."

The Marquis paused before he added,

"Therefore, because of your love of horses and your kindness to Vanessa, I am prepared to offer you his place, if you will take it."

The Chief, for the moment, seemed almost stricken.

He stared at the Marquis, as if he could not believe what he had just heard as the Marquis went on,

"If you wish to retire, if only for a little while, from the life you have been living, I can only say that my horses are the best available in this part of the country."

He smiled at the Chief before he continued,

"There is also a very nice house, which is occupied by the Head Groom in charge of them!"

"Do you really mean it, my Lord?" the Chief asked in a low voice.

"It will thank you a little for what you have done in bringing someone here who I thought I would never find. But we will talk about that later."

The Marquis turned to Melinda, who was listening wide-eyed at what was occurring and suggested,

"I think, Melinda, you should take Mr. Camden and show him the stables and the horses and find a stall for his own horse. He will be staying here with us until the Head Groom's house is available."

"Yes, yes, of course, Uncle Edward, I will do that," Melinda answered.

She moved from beside Vanessa and, as the Chief rose, she said,

"We will go out through the garden. It's much the best way to the stables. We don't want to meet that nasty old woman, which we might if we go by the front door."

Melinda ran out through the window and the Chief followed her, leaving the Marquis and Vanessa alone.

He walked towards the fireplace and stood with his back to it, as if somehow it supported him.

Vanessa rose from the table to sit on the arm of the sofa near him.

Then he said,

"I have, at least, rid you for the moment of your most unpleasant stepmother. But why did you not tell me before who you are."

"I thought that it could be dangerous for anyone to know who I really was," she replied. "You might have thought it your duty to tell my stepmother that I was here."

"I would not have done such a thing without asking your permission," he answered somewhat indignantly. "I know your father and I have always admired him. I am sure that he will welcome me as his son-in-law."

Then Vanessa looked up at him.

There was silence for a moment, until she said in a voice that he could hardly hear,

"I thought – that you were only saying it – to send Stepmama away."

The Marquis did not answer and then she went on a little more bravely,

"I thought it was – extremely clever of you to think of anything that would both surprise and shock Stepmama. At the same time I think that even when Papa comes back, I will not be able to be at home – as long as she is there."

Again there was silence and then the Marquis said,

"I thought I made it quite clear that you would stay here and I hope it will be for ever."

Vanessa rose to her feet and went nearer to him.

Her eyes, gazing into his, told him at once without words that she did not understand.

"I thought," the Marquis said very quietly, "that it was too soon to tell you what I feel about you."

He paused for a few seconds.

"But now when I have had to say it aloud, I want you to realise that I was not joking. I was merely saying something that I intended to say to you a little later when the moment was right."

"I did not – understand," Vanessa murmured.

The Marquis smiled.

"I have fallen in love," he sighed. "Head over heels in love, but I was not quite sure what you felt about me."

She looked at him and suddenly she felt very shy.

She would have turned from him, but his arms were round her and he drew her close to him.

"I have been in love with you," he said, "from the moment I first saw you. I told myself that it was absurd and you were just a Governess, but every day I wanted you more and more."

"Is that really – true?" Vanessa whispered.

The Marquis drew her closer into his arms and said,

"There is no need for words."

Then his lips sought hers.

As he kissed her, she felt something strange within her heart that she had never felt before.

It was a long kiss.

When he raised his head, she hid her face against his neck.

"Now tell me," he said in a deep voice, "what you feel about me?"

She smiled and then in a whisper Vanessa said,

"I love you. But I did not know – it was love."

"That is just what I want you to say," the Marquis said. "But tell me exactly what you are feeling."

"I only knew that I felt something so strange within me – when I saw you coming towards me. And when you kissed me – I know now it was love."

"How did you know that?" he asked.

"Because it is different from anything – I have ever felt before," she answered. "As I have never been kissed, I know that it must be my heart telling me – I am in love."

"Of course you are in love, my darling. How could you not be, when I love you more than I have ever loved anyone in my whole life?"

He paused before he went on,

"Just how could I have known? How could I have guessed that you could have transformed my naughty little niece, who every Governess told me was impossible to live with, into someone who is almost as sweet and adorable as you are?"

"That is what I want – to hear you say," Vanessa murmured.

As she looked up at him and saw the expression in his eyes, she sensed that he wanted to kiss her again.

Instinctively she raised her face nearer to his.

He kissed her until she felt that she was whirling in the sky and touching the sun.

"I love you, I love you!" she whispered. "But I did not know that – this was love."

"I will teach you, my darling, all about love and it will be the most wonderful thing I have ever done."

He kissed her again and then lifted his head to say,

"I now have a feeling that you will teach me too and, because everything you do is so original, that will be something I have never known before."

Vanessa wanted to laugh, but he was kissing her again, kissing her wildly, passionately, until they were both breathless.

Once again she hid her face against his shoulder.

She was trembling with a sublime ecstasy that she had never known in all her life.

She knew that this was what her father and mother must have felt for each other and it was what she always wanted for herself, even though she could not put it into words.

'I love you! *I love you!*' she wanted to shout out.

But it was impossible to do anything while he was kissing her.

*

They were married in the Chapel, which was at the back of the house, two days later.

The Marquis said that he did not intend to wait, even though he and Vanessa felt that they really should wait for her father's return from India.

"But if he did come to our Wedding, he would have to bring Stepmama," Vanessa reasoned, "and I could not bear her – to be there. She would be hating me and trying to make you – hate me too."

The Marquis laughed.

"That would be impossible, my precious," he said. "I know I ought to ask all my relations to the Wedding. They will be delighted that you are so lovely and that I am marrying into what they would call 'the aristocracy'."

He smiled as he added,

"But I want you all to myself."

He gave her a very tender look.

"If we get married quickly," he continued, "without all the fuss and commotion of a grand Wedding, we can slip away for our honeymoon before anyone realises what has happened."

"What about Melinda?" Vanessa asked.

"As Mr. Camden looked after you so beautifully and actually introduced us, I think we can leave Melinda in his safe hands, while we are on our honeymoon."

Vanessa smiled at him.

"I am certain," the Marquis went on, "that they will enjoy themselves racing every horse I possess and he will tell her all about the weird life he has been living. But, of course, it must be kept a secret."

"You think of everything," Vanessa sighed, "and I am only too happy to agree to everything you want."

The Marquis put his arms round her.

"All I want is you. We will forget the world and think only of love and each other until we decide to return to civilisation."

As Vanessa said to her father later, how could she refuse anything so glorious? It was so unlike anything that she had ever expected in her life.

The Chief was delighted to look after Melinda and she, for her part, was as determined as he was to try every horse in her uncle's stables.

They were the only two witnesses at the Wedding when Vanessa wore one of the most beautiful dresses that had been hidden for years in the attics at The Castle.

It was of satin and had been made for the Marquis's great-great-grandmother who had been a Princess. She had come to England at the invitation of a member of the Royal Family and fallen in love with the Marquis of that time.

The small Chapel was filled with flowers from the garden and their scent, Vanessa thought, would stay with her all the time that she was abroad.

The Marquis's private Chaplin, who was also the Vicar of the nearest village, performed the Ceremony.

He read the Service with the deepest sincerity and, when he blessed them both, Vanessa felt that they were also blessed by her mother in Heaven and by God Himself.

As they drove away to where the Marquis's yacht was waiting for them, the Chief and Melinda, hand in hand, waved until their carriage was out of sight.

The Marquis put his arms round his wife and said,

"You are not to worry. He is a very sensible man and he is delighted with Melinda, as she is with him, and they will talk horses from first thing in the morning until last thing at night!"

Vanessa laughed.

"I will not worry," she replied.

"And I will talk to you about love," the Marquis said. "A love that I thought I would never find because I knew women were always pursuing me for my title and not for myself."

"I never thought of you," Vanessa told him, "in any way except as my employer."

She smiled at him before she continued,

"It was not until you were not there that The Castle seemed empty and dull. I found myself waiting and waiting – for your return."

"And still did not know it was love?" he asked.

"Not until you kissed me," she told him. "Then I knew that the strange feelings – I had felt and the reason I was always thinking about you, was because – like you, I had fallen in love."

"I fell from the first moment I saw you. You were so sweet, so lovely and so different in every way from any woman I had ever met before."

He smiled before he added,

"How could you have been so clever as to convert Melinda from a tiresome little hooligan into the charming, attractive and very amusing young lady she is now?"

"I think I must have known that, because she was connected with you – she would also mean a great deal to me," Vanessa answered.

She gave a deep sigh before she went on,

"Oh, darling, it's so wonderful to have found you. Otherwise I might now be sitting up in the North with my relations – who had no wish to have me thrust upon them and I am sure that they would have persuaded me – that my rightful place was at home."

"You are not to think about it anymore," he said. "It was a strange way to find love. And you came into my Castle like an angel from Heaven and I knew at once that I had found at last exactly what I had always wanted, but had begun to think did not really exist."

"And that was love – real love?"

"Of course it was," he answered. "And that is what I am going to teach you, my precious. It is going to take a long time for you to learn that love is the most perfect and wonderful thing in the whole wide world and we have been fortunate enough to find it."

The Marquis kissed her again.

When they arrived at his yacht, it was to find all the beautiful clothes that the housekeeper had put on one side as her trousseau.

They had all been unpacked in the Master cabin and she thought that no one could have had a more glorious or a more historic trousseau that she had.

She knew that every dress that the housekeeper had chosen for her had its own history and came from some exciting and distinguished relation of the Marquis's in the past.

'One day I will have to write a book about them all,' Vanessa told herself.

The Marquis had already said to her,

"When we go to Paris, which we will do on our honeymoon, I will buy you an entire new trousseau."

Vanessa gave a little gasp.

"It will be the finest," the Marquis continued, "the finest that anyone will ever possess."

"I don't want anything but you!" Vanessa told him.

There were endless flowers decorating the cabin at every corner and their scent filled the air and made her feel as if she had walked into Paradise.

She realised that the large bed with its soft pillows and lace-trimmed sheets was exactly what she had thought a bride should find on her honeymoon.

As she went slowly up to the Saloon, still wearing the beautiful Wedding dress, she felt that she was moving in a dream rather than in reality.

The chef on board the yacht was French and he had excelled himself with a special dinner that Vanessa knew, when she returned to The Castle, she would have to relate to Melinda.

As she and the Marquis drank each other's health in champagne, she felt that they were drifting on a cloud up into the sky.

After dinner they went out on deck and gazed up at the moon and the stars.

Vanessa prayed that they would remain for ever as happy as they were at this magical moment.

Then they went below as the yacht moved quietly down the river towards the open sea.

The Marquis joined her a little later in the large bed in the flower-scented cabin.

He then made her completely his with a gentleness and at the same time a burning passion that could only have come from the Divine.

Vanessa felt that she was touching the stars and that God Himself was blessing them.

The Marquis knew it too.

They had found love, the real love that men and women had sought and died for since the very beginning of time.

It was the Love that came from God, was part of God and was theirs for Eternity.

Made in the USA
Middletown, DE
20 August 2023